31-
5m 3/16

THE HUCKLEBERRY MURDERS

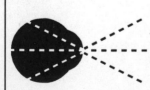

A SHERIFF BO TULLY MYSTERY

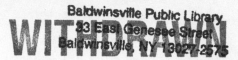

THE HUCKLEBERRY MURDERS

PATRICK F. McMANUS

THORNDIKE PRESS
A part of Gale, Cengage Learning

GALE
CENGAGE Learning™

Detroit • New York • San Francisco • New Haven, Conn • Waterville, Maine • London

GALE
CENGAGE Learning·

Copyright © 2010 by Patrick F. McManus.
Thorndike Press, a part of Gale, Cengage Learning.

Thorndike Press® Large Print Mystery.
The text of this Large Print edition is unabridged.
Other aspects of the book may vary from the original edition.
Set in 16 pt. Plantin.

LIBRARY OF CONGRESS CATALOGING-IN-PUBLICATION DATA

McManus, Patrick F.
    The huckleberry murders : a sheriff Bo Tully mystery / by
Patrick F. McManus.
        p. cm. — (Thorndike Press large print mystery)
    ISBN-13: 978-1-4104-3429-6 (hardcover)
    ISBN-10: 1-4104-3429-X (hardcover)
    1. Tully, Bo (Fictitious character)—Fiction. 2.
Sheriffs—Idaho—Fiction. 3. Ranchers—Crimes against—Fiction.
4. Idaho—Fiction. 5. Large type books. I. Title.
PS3563.C38625H83 2011
813'.54—dc22   2010046039

Published in 2011 by arrangement with Simon & Schuster, Inc.

Printed in the United States of America
1 2 3 4 5 6 7 15 14 13 12 11

To my excellent agent, Phyllis Westberg

1

Blight County, Idaho, sheriff Bo Tully drove slowly up the long gravel driveway leading to the ranch house. September had already begun, and still every day the temperature climbed into the nineties. The threat of forest fires remained. A trickle of sweat beaded up on the tip of his nose. He wiped it off. One of these days he would get the air-conditioning fixed on the Explorer. So far that summer, Blight County had managed to escape any major fires, but the mountains were powder dry. Any spark could set them off. He didn't want to think what would happen should a thunderstorm roll through. Or if his father, Pap Tully, went for a hike in the mountains smoking one of his hand-rolleds.

Tully was wearing his usual summer outfit of Levi's, long-sleeve tattersall shirt open at the collar, three-thousand-dollar alligator-hide cowboy boots, and a light khaki vest, which concealed the horizontal shoulder holster containing his 9 mm Colt Commander automatic. Today the gun seemed to weigh at least ten pounds. He preferred a lighter weapon, but criminals had become much more dangerous in recent years. He didn't believe in shooting a criminal more than twice in the body mass — the so-called double tap.

A roofed porch spread across the front of the sprawling ranch house. A man sat in a rocking chair on the porch. He had the brim of a battered cowboy hat pulled low over his eyes. Tully couldn't tell whether he was asleep or watching the vehicle approach. The man would know the red Ford Explorer belonged to law enforcement because of the light bar on the roof. He obviously was the alleged culprit the ranch owner's ex-wife had complained about.

Tully stopped the Explorer in front of the house. The man pushed the brim of his hat up with his thumb and sauntered down to greet him. He took off his hat as he approached. He appeared to be in his early thirties, slender, nice-looking, a tidy person, with short hair, a trim mustache, and under his lower lip, a tiny bush of brown hair. Tully got out of his vehicle and walked around to meet him. He stuck out his hand and said,

"Howdy, pardner, I'm Blight County sheriff Bo Tully."

The man shook his hand. "Shucks, Sheriff, I know who you are. You're the most famous person in all Blight County."

"That tells you something about Blight County, doesn't it? I take it you're Ray Crockett."

"Yep, that's me, Sheriff. No doubt Marge Poulson told you how I done away with Orville."

"She has indeed. Numerous times. So what do you have to say for yourself, Ray?"

Crockett scratched his head. "Well, let's see. I have to admit I haven't seen or heard from Orville in several months. His Social Security check arrives every month, and I mail it to a P.O. box in Spokane. Somebody picks up the checks — Orville, I suppose — and probably cashes them. That post office box would be pretty full by now if nobody picked up the checks."

"Sounds like a reasonable guess. How long have you been mailing his checks to Spokane?"

Crockett squinted up, as if looking for the answer in the sky. "Quite a while. Going on a couple of years."

"You have an address or phone number for Orville?"

9

"Nope, I don't. He travels a lot and stays in hotels. He used to call me every couple weeks or so, but now months go by I don't hear from him."

"What do you do for a living, Ray?"

Crockett put his hat back on. "Not much, Sheriff. Orville lets me stay here free of charge to look after the ranch, but he sold off all the stock so there's not much to look after. I helped him sell the stock and he gave me five percent of the gross. I put my share in a CD. Then my dad died and I got a bit of insurance money. That's mostly what I've been living on." He gestured toward the ranch house. "This is a nice place to live and I guess I'll stay here till Orville tells me different or my money runs out. I'm not one of those people consumed by ambition but lately I been thinking about taking some courses at the community college. Do something with my life."

"You have a major in mind?"

"I've been thinking maybe law."

"Never can tell when that might come in handy. So, any other plans, Ray?"

"Haven't made up my mind yet. I guess I'll stick on here until Marge gets on my nerves so much I can't stand it. Small wonder Orville divorced her! Grab a seat up on the porch, Sheriff, and I'll go fetch us each a beer."

Tully pursed his lips, as if considering the offer. "Sounds mighty tempting, Ray, but I've got to get moving on. Give me the address of that Spokane mailbox, will you?"

"Sure thing. I have to go in the house to get it. My memory's like a sieve."

"Mine too. Write it down for me, would you, Ray?"

Tully looked around at the farm buildings. He made out a large boat in an open shed and behind it a barn that had probably once been cadmium red but now had faded with age into a weathered burnt sienna. No, that wasn't quite it. Tully felt the urge to give up on law enforcement once and for all and start painting full-time.

Crockett returned with the mailbox address written down on a piece of blue-lined paper apparently torn out of a small notebook. He handed it to Tully.

"Thanks, Ray. I'll check it out. Maybe that will satisfy Marge and get her off my back. Maybe even off your back."

"That would be nice." Crockett's thumb stroked the bit of fuzz under his lip. "If I can be of any more help, Sheriff, let me know. The next time Orville calls, I'll have him get in touch. The last I heard from him, though, he said he was headed down to

11

Mexico. I figure he must be having a pretty good time down there because I haven't heard from him since."

Tully nodded. "When was the last time you mailed his Social Security check to Spokane?"

"Just a couple days ago."

"How old is he now, late sixties?"

"Sounds about right. He was in great shape the last time I saw him."

"You a fisherman, Ray?"

"No, afraid not. Fishing is one of the few vices I've never tried. Why do you ask?"

Tully pointed at the boat.

"Oh, that. It belongs to Orville. He used to spend a lot of time out on Lake Blight. Said he knew the lake like the back of his hand. He was always bringing home messes of fish. Don't ask what kind because I don't know."

"That's about the biggest Boston Whaler I've ever seen. Looks like an outboard jet motor for power."

"I don't know one boat from another, Sheriff."

"Well, thanks for your help, Ray. If you hear from Poulson, let me know."

"You got it, Sheriff."

Tully got in his Explorer, drove around the circular drive, and headed back toward the highway, tugging thoughtfully on the corner of his mustache. In his rearview mirror he watched Crockett return to his chair and tilt the hat down over his eyes, apparently to resume his nap. He appeared to be a nice young man, polite, attentive, respectful. In other words, a classic sociopath. He lied as smoothly as if he were telling the truth. Marge was right. Ray killed the old man. The questions were, what did he do with the body, and how does he cash Orville's Social Security checks?

A fly walked across the inside of his windshield. He decided to let it live. It could suffer in the heat along with him.

2

It was now almost noon. He decided to swing by his mother's house and see what she was making for lunch.

He rapped on her front door and then walked in. Katherine Rose McCarthy Tully O'Hare Tully Casey stuck her head out of the kitchen. "I've been expecting you, Bo. I made lunch for both of us. I'm still getting fresh tomatoes, so I made us BLTs and Campbell's chicken noodle soup."

"Sounds perfect." As he walked toward the kitchen he noticed a framed, sepia-tinted wedding photo on an end table next to the sofa, Rose and his father, Pap. Tully had a hard time remembering his mother's four marriages, two of them to his father, a former and much-feared sheriff of Blight County. Maybe Pap was back in her good graces.

Rose apparently had just got a new hairdo. He preferred her white, but this short bob with a brown tint did make her look younger. "So what are you up to today, Bo?"

He kissed her on the cheek. "I'll tell you but I don't want it blabbed all over town." He slid into a chair at the kitchen table, pulled the Colt Commander from its shoulder holster, and laid it on the linoleum. Rose hated eating with him when he was armed.

She said, "Heaven forbid I would do such a thing."

"I mean it, Ma! I tell you about my cases only because you lead such a dull life. In this instance I'm pretty sure I'm dealing with a killer."

"He murdered someone!" Her eyes lit up. "You know I love murders best, Bo!"

"Yeah, that's why I'll tell you. But you better not utter a peep about this to anyone, you understand, or it will be the last murder you hear!"

"Cross my heart." Rose set a bowl of soup in front of him and a plate of BLT halves in the middle of the table. She had toasted the bread and cut the sandwiches into triangles. Bo sampled a BLT. For all of her hell-raising youth, Rose had somehow managed to become a good cook, at least as far as BLTs were concerned. She was pretty good with Campbell's chicken noodle soup, too.

15

"Okay then, here's the situation, Ma. An elderly rancher disappeared about two years ago. Nobody has heard from him in months except the young fellow running his ranch. The rancher's ex is sure he's been murdered."

Rose was about to bite into her BLT but stopped. "The wife did it!"

"That's certainly possible. But until I find the body, I can't be sure he's been murdered at all. His widow once removed, if she is one, thinks it's the fellow taking care of the ranch who did Orville in."

"Orville! You're talking about Orville Poulson! I know both the Poulsons, Orville and Marge! They're a wonderful couple! Marge certainly isn't the kind of person to kill her ex-husband, unless the husband was someone like Pap, and I can assure you he isn't, or wasn't, as the case may be. She's a very nice lady."

"Let's leave my father out of this. You're the one who said the wife did it." Tully helped himself to another BLT.

Rose sniffed. "That was before I knew we were talking about the Poulsons."

"Anyway, I don't have a body and I don't have a clue where to look for one. That ranch is huge. Orville could be buried anywhere on it."

16

Rose sipped her soup, slurped in a noodle, then dabbed her lips with a napkin. "Well, that's hardly a problem. You just go ask Mrs. Gorsich where the body is."

"Mrs. Gorsich! You think she did it? At the very least, I should arrest her for telling fortunes without a license."

"There's a license for fortune-telling?"

"I don't know. I guess not. I should put her in jail anyway. Maybe for taking money under false pretenses!" One of his main pleasures in life was to tease his mother.

"False pretenses, my eye! Bo, she's a real psychic! She taps into the spirit world and can tell both the past and the future! You go ask her and she'll tell you where poor Orville is buried."

"I find Mrs. Gorsich to be more of a physic than a psychic."

"That's all you know. Half the businessmen in town won't make a major decision without consulting Etta first."

"Why do I find that so easy to believe? Can you imagine what the commissioners would say if I turned in a bill for consulting a fortune-teller?"

"They would be pleased as punch, Bo, to find out the Sheriff's Department was finally using some common sense to solve crimes."

"Hmm. Knowing the commissioners as I do, I think you're probably right about that. Just to satisfy you, I tell you what. I'll go check out this Mrs. Gorsich." He pushed his chair away from the table with a sigh. "Anyway, the lunch is perfect. You make a great BLT, Ma."

"I have many talents, Bo, many talents."

He nodded at her hair. "Your new do looks terrific, by the way."

Rose beamed at the compliment. "Makes me look younger, doesn't it?"

"Oh yeah. Just to warn you, if I see any young bucks hanging around here, I'm going to throw them in jail. Maybe you, too!"

Tully got back to the department shortly after one o'clock. His staff was hard at work, probably because they had heard the *klock-klock* approach of his boot heels on the marble-chip floor. He wasn't surprised to see his undersheriff, Herb Eliot, still reading the day's *Blight Bugle,* with an intensity that suggested he was looking for clues to the day's crimes. How Herb could find so much to read in the paper Tully couldn't imagine.

The Crime Scene Investigations Unit — Byron "Lurch" Proctor — was bent over his computer in the corner. The corner space

18

was exclusively his. Lurch thought of it as his lab. Tully had given him his nickname, Lurch. Even so, the sheriff was Lurch's hero. The CSI Unit was possibly the world's homeliest human being, with dull brown hair that stuck mostly straight up, a nose much too large for his face, rimless glasses half an inch thick perched atop the nose, floppy ears, and beady eyes. But he was brilliant. Besides that, his girlfriend, Sarah, was not only the most gorgeous young woman Tully had ever seen, she was also the smartest, a scientist who worked for a Boise hospital. Tully had begun to think maybe there was something to be said for homely. Oh, yeah, as long as you were brilliant, too.

Daisy Quinn, Bo's secretary and also a deputy, extremely compact and pretty, with close-cut curly black hair and brown eyes, was a woman who fairly exuded efficiency. Tully had recently made the mistake of having a brief fling with Daisy, a mistake that conceivably could have gotten both him and Daisy fired. Nevertheless, she had helped him over what Tully thought of as a rough patch and he now appreciated Daisy more than ever, even though he tried to make a point of not showing it. During his absences, he let his undersheriff, Herb, think he ran the department, but Daisy actually was the one in charge. All his deputies knew to take their orders from the secretary. Daisy brooked no nonsense from them.

Tully stuck his head into the radio room and said hi to Flo, his radio person. She gave him her usual big smile. Florence "Flo" Getts was his go-to person whenever Daisy wasn't available. Undersheriff Herb Eliot was so far down on the list, Tully often forgot about him, even if the department was extremely busy. He had long ago figured out that in any business, institution, or other kind of organization, there was always at least one totally useless person. Usually it was a person high up the organizational chart, if not at the top. He sometimes wondered if headhunters didn't advertise for totally useless people. This was the position for which Herb was totally qualified.

"Hey, Lurch!" Tully yelled across the briefing room.

Lurch looked up from his computer and gave him a big grin. "Hey, Bo!"

"I've got some work for you." He walked over to the Unit and handed him the piece of paper Crockett had given him. "See if you can find some prints on this — other than mine, that is. If you find any, run them through IAFIS and see if you can find a match."

20

"IAFIS" stood for "Integrated Automated Fingerprint Identification System."

"You got it, Bo. Shouldn't take long."

Tully walked over to his glassed-in office. "Daisy, bring your pad. I've got some work for you, too."

She got up from her desk and bustled in. "How did I ever guess?"

"Beats me. You must be psychic. Which reminds me, you know anything about this Etta Gorsich?"

"The fortune-teller? I've never met Gorsich but there are people in town who swear by her. I've heard all kinds of stories about how she's contacted dead relatives and come up with messages from them, that sort of thing. Weird stuff. You wouldn't get me within a thousand yards of that house of hers."

"Really? I was thinking of sending you over there for a reading, or whatever they call it."

"No way!"

Tully leaned back in his chair. "What does she look like, Daisy? Skip the part about a pointed black hat and a broom."

"I've never seen her. I don't think she leaves that creepy house of hers very often. She doesn't make house calls, as far as I know. You have to go to her if you want

21

whatever she has to sell. I can feel the hair rising on the back of my neck just talking about her."

Tully smiled. He couldn't believe a person as sensible as Daisy could be affected by such nonsense. "Well, if you refuse to check her out, I guess maybe I'll drift over there after work. I had no idea you're such a chicken, Daisy."

She laughed. "I'll be waiting for your report first thing in the morning, Sheriff."

3

Etta Gorsich's house sat by itself atop a steep but low hill. It was surrounded by overgrown trees, brush, dried grass, weeds, and dead wildflowers, mostly daisies, dandelions, and thistles. Apparently, the fortune-teller wasn't big on landscaping. He climbed the steep, rickety wooden stairs leading to the front porch. Tully ignored the two handrails on principle. He thought they were mostly for sissies. The front porch looked as if it had recently been worked on, here and there a new board showing fresh and clean. Tully, already nervous and regretting his decision to check out Mrs. Gorsich, started to knock on the door. It popped open before his knuckles made the first rap.

An attractive middle-aged woman stood there smiling at him. She was in fact one of the better-looking women Tully had seen in a long while. He instantly regretted jumping back and gasping "Whoa!" at the suddenness of the door springing open. She wore a cream-colored tailored suit on her slim, shapely figure and a necklace of pearls around her elegant neck. Her smile was large and gleamed with both amusement and sparkling white teeth. "Hello," she said in a husky voice.

"Uh, hello," Tully managed. "I'm Blight County sheriff Bo Tully and —"

"I know who you are, Sheriff. Everyone in Blight County knows Sheriff Bo Tully. Please come in. I hope you're not here to investigate the ridiculous rumors that I'm some kind of fortune-teller."

"Uh," Tully said.

"Please have a seat over on the sofa, Sheriff. I was just making a pot of tea. Would you like some?"

"Uh," Tully said again.

"A cup of tea?" the woman said. "Would you like one?"

"Why, thank you," Tully blurted as if coming out of a coma. "A cup of tea sounds great."

Mrs. Gorsich disappeared into what Tully assumed was the kitchen. He walked over to the sofa and sat down. The room appeared to be expensively and tastefully decorated. If the lady made her money from fortune-telling, she apparently did very well at it. Tully tapped his finger nervously on his knee and waited for her to return.

Mrs. Gorsich presently came out of the kitchen with a tray containing a silver teapot, two china cups on saucers, two silver teaspoons, a small pitcher of cream, and a crystal bowl of raw sugar, a tiny spoon sticking out of it. She placed the tray on the coffee table and sat down in a chair across from him. She had excellent posture, her back perfectly straight. He would have to tell his mother about Mrs. Gorsich's posture. Rose had a thing about posture.

"So, Sheriff, did you bring your handcuffs?"

"Uh, no. No, I didn't bring any handcuffs."

"Too bad. It might have been interesting."

Tully stared at her, his mind now a complete blank.

Mrs. Gorsich laughed. "Only joshing you, Sheriff. I'm sorry. Please tell me why you're here." She poured the tea.

Tully put two tiny spoonfuls of raw sugar in his tea, stirred in some cream, and took a long sip, all the time trying to think of why he was there.

"Basically," he finally said, "I guess I'm here because I try to know all the residents of Blight County, particularly those about whom I hear rumors."

" 'Whom'!" Mrs. Gorsich exclaimed. "Sheriff, you are the first person in Blight County I've heard use the word 'whom' — at least, to do so correctly. You obviously are an educated person."

"I had a very mean English professor in college, Dr. Agatha Wrenn. We were terrified of her. Learning proper grammar seemed the safest thing to do. If you said 'snuck' for 'sneaked,' you were taken out behind the language arts building and shot."

"Maybe that's why you went into law enforcement after college."

"It was pretty much expected of me. Men in my family have been Blight County sheriffs for the last hundred years. But I'm here to find out about you, Mrs. Gorsich."

She refilled his cup. "Etta, please. You mean about my being a fortune-teller?" She laughed. "I admit that many Blight City businessmen come to me for advice about decisions they have to make. They are simple folk for the most part, and I'm sure they think of me as a fortune-teller, particularly when my advice works out for them. I'm actually a financial consultant. I have an MBA from an Ivy League university, the name of which would be too pretentious of me to mention. I worked on the Street for a dozen years and was quite successful at it."

Tully couldn't believe she had just confessed to having been a prostitute.

She apparently read the puzzlement on his face. "Wall Street," she said.

"Oh, right."

"So, you're wondering why I ended up here. Well, I didn't end up here. I may move on at any time, but I've become very fond of Idaho. It's a beautiful state, and the people are nice, and I just have a sense of peace here. Anytime I get bored I fly off to San Francisco or New York, but it's not long before I come zipping back to Idaho. I have quite a list of clients here I help with investments."

"I could never leave Idaho," Tully said. "So I'm not surprised you like it."

He set his empty teacup back on the tray. He couldn't remember having drunk any of the tea. Etta Gorsich picked up the teapot and refilled his cup. There was something about the woman that soaked up his total attention.

"I understand, Sheriff, that you are a very successful artist."

Tully laughed. "That all depends upon what you mean by 'very.' I've been painting most of my life and tend to view the world more as a painter than as a sheriff. Only in

27

very recent years have my paintings started to sell. My hope is one day to give up sheriffing and become a poor but otherwise modestly successful full-time artist."

He set his cup back on the tray and pushed himself up from the couch. "I'd better not take up any more of your time, Mrs. Gorsich. Thank you very much for the tea."

"Please, call me Etta," she said, smiling, pouring him another cup of tea. "And is it all right if I call you Bo?"

"Sure," he said, settling back on the couch. "Everybody does, even my criminals."

"I hope you don't think of me as one of your criminals."

"Not at all." He sipped his tea.

Etta said, "I've traveled all over the world, Bo, and met hundreds of interesting people, but I have to say, you are the most interesting man I've come across in a long while."

Tully didn't know what to say. Finally, he managed to get out a modest "Well, uh, thank you. No one has ever said that to me before. I suppose maybe they didn't notice."

"Oh, I'm sure they noticed."

After a bit more conversation, he picked up his teacup, only to notice she had refilled it again. He set the cup back on the tray and stood up. "I really shouldn't take up any more of your time."

Etta stood and walked him to the door. "Please come again, Bo."

"You can count on that, Etta."

He turned to thank her again for her time. She came up close and put her hand on his chest. Tully thought she had stopped his heart.

"Next time, Bo," she said, "don't forget the handcuffs."

Tully fumbled with the doorknob, finally got it to turn in the right direction. He went out onto the porch and started down the steps. He knew Rose would be disappointed that he hadn't asked Mrs. Gorsich about Orville's body.

"Oh, Sheriff!" Etta called after him.

Tully stopped and turned.

"Look under the house!"

Tully gave her a brief smile and continued on down the steps. It was only at the bottom he realized he had been using both handrails.

For the first time in his life, he had met a woman he didn't think he could manage. She was like some kind of space alien, dropped into Blight City to spy on the populace. She would no doubt report back to her managers, some form of reptiles who would at some point descend on Blight and eat all the residents. To investigate her more thoroughly, he should invite Etta to lunch. He might even throw some really tough grammar at her. His tough grammar bounced undetected off local women, but Etta would be different,

He went back to the courthouse and down to the jail in the basement to check on his usual suspects. Sometimes the criminals got a little rowdy and had to be settled down. A riot or anything seriously dangerous he left to his jail matron, Lulu Cobb. Lulu's reputation was such that she had to do nothing more than open the cell-block door and yell, "All right, you idiots, knock it off — you don't want me down there with my stick!"

Tully had never seen her down there with her stick, and it was a sight he seriously wished to avoid. Tully himself took a much softer line toward the inmates. Most of them were young and stupid, and he thought maybe Lulu reminded them of their mothers.

He found her at her desk outside the cell-block door. A partially played hand of solitaire was spread out on the wood top of the battered desk. "How are our critters, Lulu?"

She shoved herself up. "Oh, they get a

little restless along about feeding time, but they been quiet enough. You want to go in and visit with them, Bo?"

"I guess not, Lulu. My stomach is a little queasy today. Maybe tomorrow. Be careful."

"I'm always careful, Bo, always careful."

He tromped up the two sets of stairs and down the hall toward his office. The daytime shift had already left the briefing room, Herb and Daisy among them, but Lurch was still hard at work in his corner. Tully sometimes thought maybe Lurch had no other life, but then it would occur to him that the Unit had the beautiful Sarah. And Sarah was a major something.

"Hey, Lurch!" hc yelled.

"Hey, Bo!"

"You get any prints off that paper?"

"Yeah, I got a match, too."

"So don't keep me in suspense."

Lurch thumbed through a notepad next to his computer.

"To begin with, his name isn't Ray Crockett."

"Big surprise."

"His name is Ray Porter. He did two years for possession with intent to sell. Got out in 2002. Since then he's been clean, at least as far as law enforcement knows."

"Right. As far as we know."

Lurch smiled. "I hear you checked on Mrs. Gorsich. How did that go?"

"Daisy has a big mouth. Yes, I went up and met Etta Gorsich. She's a very nice lady — attractive, too. And sophisticated. Not at all what I expected. Her so-called fortune-telling is nothing more than business advice. She's an investment consultant, not a fortune-teller."

"How good-looking is she?"

"I'm inviting her to lunch."

"That good, huh?"

"Almost up to Sarah's level, but a few years older."

Lurch feigned amazement. "Wow, that's dynamite, boss. I was wondering what it might be like to date a fortune-teller. She would always know what you're thinking."

"Women always know what we're thinking, Lurch. But one last time, she's not a fortune-teller."

"Right, boss." The Unit gave him one of his snaggle-toothed grins and went back to his computer.

Tully stepped into his office to look at some papers Daisy had left for him. He flopped into his chair and began aimlessly tapping his fingers on the desk. Suddenly he stopped. *Look under the house!* What on earth had she meant by that? The hair stirred on the back of his neck.

4

Tully took the next day off. It was getting late in the season for huckleberries but he wanted to get some digital photos of them for his files and maybe a gallon or so for huckleberry pie and pancakes. He had picked and eaten huckleberries all his life. Lately it had occurred to him that he actually didn't like huckleberries all that much. What motivated him to pick them every year? Maybe it was because they were free and all you had to do was go out in the woods and pick them.

He had been working on a painting of a chipmunk perched on a weathered log and had decided some huckleberries in the foreground would lend a nice touch. He had picked and eaten many thousands of huckleberries, but when it came to painting rather than eating, he couldn't seem to get them right. Besides, he felt like a long drive in the mountains. This late in the season, he knew if he were to find berries, it would have to be in the high country. With the economy scraping bottom, there were so many commercial pickers they cleaned out just about every berry, so there was hardly anything left for the ordinary picker. He hoped they hadn't found his secret patch, up on the back of Scotchman Peak. He didn't need many huckleberries for his photograph, but it would be nice if he could take Rose back enough for a couple of pies.

Having donned his lucky picking clothes, still stained with blotches of faded purple from many seasons and many washings, he added a khaki vest to conceal his Colt Commander. There had been a time when it never would have occurred to him to take a gun with him to pick huckleberries. But this was a different world, a different time.

He drove his battered 1985 blue pickup truck up along Scotchman Peak Road, his metal berry pickers and two gallon-size pails rattling in a cardboard box next to him. Finally he came to the steep grade that went up over Henrys Pass. Nearing the top of the grade, his rear tires began to spin on loose shale and gravel. When he reached the little road leading to his secret patch, he parked and turned the hubs on the front wheels, engaging the four-wheel drive. As he climbed back into the truck a faint chorus of screams reached him. The old logging road ran along the slope of the mountain off to his left. He walked over and peered in the direction of the screams. A green Chevy Suburban was parked a couple of hundred yards down the road. A dead tree lay in front of it. He got into his truck, drove down to the Suburban, and got out. The screams were moving toward him. He could tell they came from women, no doubt huckleberry pickers who had run into a bear. The bear was probably racing for his life over the top of the mountain. The ladies came around a curve in the road and were now huffing and puffing toward him, their huckleberry pails bouncing about from belts tied loosely around their waists. He leaned against the Suburban and waited.

There were five of them, three matronly types and two younger ones. They gathered around him, all too breathless to talk. They kept pointing back down the logging road. He scanned the woods on both sides of the road, hoping not to see an irritable grizzly charging in his direction.

"Oh, Sheriff Tully!" gasped a plump gray-haired lady with a red bandanna tied loosely around her neck. "Are we ever glad to see you!"

Tully smiled at her. "What seems to be the trouble, Blanche?"

"Bodies!" blurted out a younger blond woman, perspiration streaming down her reddened face.

"Bodies?" Tully said. "What kind of bodies?"

"Dead bodies!" blurted another one.

"Dead bodies all over the place!" cried another woman, who looked as if she were about to be sick. The women were now all leaning against the Suburban. He hoped none of them was going to faint.

He peered off down the road. "Exactly where are these bodies?"

One of the ladies pointed. "Down around that bend."

Tully studied the group. They looked relatively sane. "Okay, ladies, you all get in your vehicle and rest, but don't leave. I may need your names, addresses, and phone numbers." He took a pen and small notebook from his shirt pocket. "You can write them in here while you're waiting."

He walked down the road, watching for any movement ahead of him. Reaching under his vest as he moved around the bend, he unsnapped the strap retaining the Colt Commander. The dry grass along the edge of the road had grown up knee high

37

and he had no trouble finding where the ladies had matted it down. He stepped off the road and began working his way down the slope toward a mass of huckleberry bushes. Three bodies lay on their bellies at the edge of the patch. They had ropes around their waists, maybe to hold berry buckets they were now lying on. He sat down on a stump and studied them. All had been shot in the back of the head. Each of them wore sneakers, now barely holding together, and pants and shirts in scarcely better condition. Clearly, they hadn't been killed for their money. He got up and lifted one of the hands. It was callused and darkened, probably from hard labor involving dirt. They appeared to be laborers of some kind, probably from a farm of some sort. None appeared older than twenty. He pulled one of the victims up slightly so he could see beneath him. As he expected, a two-pound coffee can had been outfitted with a wire bale. A length of rope ran around the picker's waist and through the bale.

Weird, Tully thought. All three had apparently intended to pick berries when someone shot them in the back of the head. There must have been three shooters. Otherwise at least one of the victims would have spun around at the first shot or reacted in some way. They were lying in a perfect line. He imagined himself as one of the young men headed down toward the berry patch. Why does someone haul you up in the woods to pick huckleberries? If he had been one of the intended victims, he would have sensed something funny from the start. The minute his feet hit the ground he would have run like a spooked deer down the side of the mountain. If there were three shooters, the three intended victims would have died instantly and simultaneously. On the other hand, if there was a fourth intended victim, it was possible he had managed to escape. Tully got up and walked down through an opening in the brush, examining leaves as he went. On the lower side of the berry patch he found what he was looking for. A tiny spot of dried blood glistened on a leaf. Maybe the fourth intended victim was lying dead somewhere down on the steep slope of the mountain. Or maybe, somehow, miraculously, he had gotten away. Tully worked his way back to the road. This was the worst case of cold-blooded murder he had encountered in his entire career in law enforcement. He noticed that his hands were shaking. He squeezed them into fists as he walked back to the Suburban.

Blanche, the apparent leader of the group, handed him the notebook. The ladies seemed exhausted. Tully suspected they had picked their last huckleberry. He checked the notebook to make sure they had included all the information he had asked for. They had. He walked back to his pickup and backed it out onto the main road so the Suburban could get by. After pulling back into the logging road, he stopped halfway to the dead tree, took out his cell phone, and called Lurch.

"Yeah, boss," the Unit answered. Tully suspected Lurch received phone calls only from him.

"Lurch, I'm up here on Scotchman Peak Road, about a mile from Henrys Pass. I've got three dead bodies in a huckleberry patch. They've each been shot in the back of the head. So bring your kit and a metal detector. We might be able to find some shell casings. Call Dave Perkins at the House of Fry and tell him I need him up here, too."

There was no reply.

"Lurch, you there?"

"Yeah. Give me a second. Three bodies. Dave? How come Dave?"

"He's probably the best tracker in the entire country."

"You think the killer might still be around?"

"No, but I need Dave up here."

"How about Pap?"

Tully thought for a moment. The old man relished any chance to relive his sheriff days and would never forgive him if he were left out of a triple murder. "Yeah, tell Dave to pick up Pap on his way." Then he remembered the medical examiner. "Call the M.E. and tell her we need her whole outfit up here. Tell Susan we've got three bodies, maybe a fourth."

"A fourth!" Lurch let a long breath sizzle through his teeth. "Right, boss."

5

Tully had heard a logging truck go by earlier, so he walked out to the main road. He sat down on a large rock to wait for the next truck. Presently he could hear it growling down a steep slope up near the pass. It soon came swaying around the bend with a massive load of logs. He got up and waved his arms. The driver started working his way down through the gears and pulled up next to Tully with a hiss and squeal of brakes.

"Bo!" the driver said. "What the devil you doing out here?"

Tully climbed up on the running board. "Pete, I was trying to pick some huckleberries," he said, "but before I could get to it, I found three young guys out there in the brush, all of them shot in the back of the head."

Pete gasped out an obscenity. "What's the world coming to, Bo? Even way up here in the mountains you got folks getting themselves murdered!"

"As to what the world is coming to, I wish I knew, but I don't. Have you heard any shots the last few days?"

"Can't say I have. Oh, you know grouse season is open and occasionally we hear somebody popping off at one of them."

"Yeah, I suppose. I suspect revolvers were used. Otherwise, the casings would have been flying off into the brush and hard if not impossible for the killers to find. I figure there had to be three shooters. I've got Lurch headed up here with a metal detector, and maybe we can find some casings, if the shooters were using automatics."

Pete said, "We got trucks driving this road constantly, and I'll spread the word to the other drivers. Maybe one of them heard some shots. There's a driver either going up or down this road about every half hour. I'll pass the word, see if anybody's heard or seen anything."

"Thanks, Pete. They may know something useful." Tully dropped back to the ground. Pete gave him a little wave, and the truck went growling down the mountain.

Two hours later a caravan of cars came streaming up the road. Tully had built a small castle of rocks and was trying to think of something else to do when they finally arrived. He directed them into the logging road and walked up to the head of the line. They stopped behind his pickup, a hundred feet in front of the dead tree. It was possible Lurch might be able to find some tread imprints from the shooters' tires in that hundred feet, even though the women's Suburban had been driven all the way to the tree. A couple of state patrolmen had joined the group, as well as a U.S. forest ranger. Susan arrived in a coroner's van, trailed by another van. Stepping out the passenger door, she gave him one of her special smiles. They still hadn't gotten back together after their last breakup, a result of Tully's failure to be sufficiently attentive. Oh, yeah, and there had also been his brief affair with Daisy. That was before he made Daisy a deputy and issued her a department gun. It had later occurred to him that it wasn't such a good idea to issue a gun to a woman with whom you had broken up. He had so many women in his life he might have to hire a secretary to keep track of them. Then he would probably end up having an affair with the secretary. That's how his life went these days. Not bad, actually.

"Hey, Susan!" he said. "You get to go first." He pointed down the slope in the direction of the bodies. "If you need some help with your stuff, I'll haul it down for you."

She grinned at him. "I know, you're just trying to be attentive, Bo, but I've got some helpers along." She looked down the slope at the bodies and shook her head. "This is just so terrible!"

"Yeah." He remained on the road. Observing medical examiners at their work was not on his list of favorite activities.

Lurch hauled his metal detector over. Tully pointed out where he thought the shooters must have stood, and the Unit began sweeping the instrument back and forth. Nothing. "Looks as if they picked up their casings, boss. Or maybe they were using revolvers."

"Give it another pass down the slope a ways."

Lurch walked a few steps down toward the bodies, swinging the detector back and forth. The instrument beeped.

"What is it?" Tully asked.

Lurch bent down and picked up the object. "A bottle cap." He cocked his arm as if to throw the cap off into the brush.

"Stop!" Tully yelled. "Let me see it."

Lurch climbed back up the slope and handed him the cap. "You think the killers took time out to share a beer?"

"Who knows?" Tully looked at the cap. "It's a twist-off, Lurch. Dos Equis. Mexican beer. Look around and see if you can find the bottle. We could get fingerprints off the bottle. If you can't find a Dos Equis bottle here, I want you to check the brush on each side of the road all the way back to that downed tree."

Lurch shook his head. "You want to arrest these killers for littering?"

"Just see if you can find me the bottle, Lurch!"

"Maybe I can get a print off the cap, Bo."

"Just find me the bottle! The guy twists the cap off the bottle here and starts drinking his beer on the way back to his car. When the bottle is empty, he tosses it out into the brush."

"Jeez, boss, I'd have to scour ten acres of brush!"

"What else do you have to do? You want to go help Susan?"

"Only kidding. I'll go look for the bottle." He sighed and started scanning the brush.

"If you find it, Lurch, don't mess up any possible prints."

"Thanks, boss. I'd never have thought of that."

Dave Perkins came walking up. He wore a buckskin shirt, jeans, and moccasins. His

46

long gray hair hung in a thick braid down his back.

"I see you're wearing your tracking clothes," Tully said.

"Yeah, they help me concentrate." He glanced down at Susan and the three bodies. "Some really bad people running around nowadays. Maybe there always were. These guys look pretty young."

Tully nodded. "Yeah, I figure none of them is over twenty. No ID on any of them, at least that I could find. I did check their hands. Lots of calluses. I make them out to be farm laborers."

"Latinos?"

"Nope, all gringos, far as I can tell. They've been doing some hard labor, though, and I don't think they've been paid much, if anything. Their clothes are barely holding together."

Dave squinted down at Susan, then jerked his head around and gave an exaggerated shudder. "I can't believe you once dated her, Bo."

"Yeah, it was rough duty, particularly when she rehashed her day's activities while we were having supper."

"So what do you want from me, Sheriff?"

Tully told him about the possibility of an intended fourth victim who may have got-

47

ten away. "If I had been one of the intended vics, I'd have been very suspicious of anyone who took me up to pick huckleberries. At the first shot I would have taken off and run like a deer. So I walked down through the berry patch and found a tiny spot of blood on a branch down there. If one guy did get away, he may have been hit pretty hard, but I don't think so. Still, it's possible you'll find his body down the slope somewhere. On the other hand, if he was only nicked by the bullet, maybe he's alive and out there someplace. If we find him alive, we'll nail the killers."

"It's possible," Dave said. "Won't hurt for me to take a look in any case."

"You come up with Pap?"

"Yeah." He jerked his thumb in the direction of his truck.

Tully looked back down the road but couldn't see his father. "I'll have him drive your rig back to town. Once you've cut the track, if there is one, mark it and head out to the road. I'll pick you up on my way back into town."

Dave nodded. He circled far out around Susan and the victims and headed down the slope, zigzagging back and forth in order to cut the track, if there was one. Tully watched him until he was out of sight.

Pap came ambling up the road and stood beside him. He wore jeans, a denim work shirt open at the collar, cowboy boots, and a khaki vest similar to his son's. His thick white hair was cropped close to the scalp. The old man had been out of law enforcement for over ten years but he seemed as fit as ever. "A triple murder! You have all the luck, Bo."

"Yeah, don't I?"

Pap stared down at the bodies. "I see you got Susan up here already, along with most of the county. Everybody loves a murder, and here you land a triple. In all my years as sheriff, I didn't have but two triples."

"One that you committed?"

Pap blurted out an obscenity. "Those were three bank robbers and you know it! I killed them fair and square! Got plugged three times myself and even was awarded a commendation from the governor."

"I believe you've mentioned that to me a few hundred times. What was the other triple?"

"You made me mad, Bo, so I ain't going to tell you."

Tully glanced at his father. The old man was tall and lean, his skin deeply tanned from a lifetime of hunting and fishing and roaming the mountains. "Tell me," he said.

49

He knew the old man couldn't resist.

"They was all gamblers. They cooked up a scheme to rip off one of the joints. Not a good idea. It was one of the few crimes I never solved."

"That because you had an interest in the joint?"

Pap laughed. "That's for me to know. I see you've notified just about everybody in the entire state, Bo. So I was wondering why the FBI hasn't showed up."

"The FBI? Why should I notify them?"

"This is a national forest. The last time I looked, national forests were on federal land. The FBI usually likes to investigate murders on federal land."

"Is that right? I didn't know. Well, as soon as I get back to town, I'll have to give them a call. If I don't forget. So why do you think these fellows might have been killed?"

"A killing like this, Bo, you got to figure it's about money."

"You think these fellows were done for money?"

"Somebody wanted to dispose of them, that's pretty obvious. The question is why. You usually dispose of a person because you don't want him blabbing something he knows about you. These fellers look pretty young, from what I can see of them. It's

50

doubtful any of them knew enough of anything to get them killed. So what does that leave?"

"Beats the heck out of me."

"You're so dumb, Bo. The only other sensible reason to kill a person is money."

"I don't think these guys had any money at all."

"Maybe they was killed to keep them that way. And maybe to keep them quiet, too."

"You may be right."

6

By late afternoon, the bodies had been loaded into the coroner's vans to be hauled back to Susan's lab. She stood at the edge of the road, her face glistening with sweat, a wisp of hair stuck to her cheek. "I have to find another line of work," she told Tully.

"Can't blame you for that," he said. "So, can you tell me when they were killed?"

"Right now all I can tell you is, within the last couple of days, because —"

"Skip the details, please! Just give me your best estimate."

"That is my best estimate, Bo. I'll be able to narrow down the time once I get them back to the lab. If any of them has a record, you might be able to get an ID from his prints. My guess is that at least one of them has been arrested for something one time or another. You usually don't meet guys at a church social who wind up shooting you in the back."

Tully tugged on the corner of his mustache. "Yeah, I guess you're right about that. Print them for me, please, and I'll see if Lurch can find a match."

"I'll get them over to Byron tonight. Since you keep him working night and day, you might have at least one ID by tomorrow."

Tully laughed. "Sounds as if you've been listening to Lurch complain. Which reminds me, I've got him checking out a partial tire track as well as looking for a beer bottle."

Susan shook her head and climbed into the passenger side of the last van to back out. Other hangers-on had left the scene earlier. A few were standing around in groups out on the Scotchman Peak Road. The Unit came walking up carrying a plaster cast.

"You able to get anything we can use, Lurch?"

"Maybe. The lady pickers' car pretty much rolled over the top of the lower track, but I was able to cast several inches on the edge. The vehicle that made the lower track had very wide tires. Could even be dual tires. Probably made from the shooters' tires because the track looks just a bit older than the Suburban's. Has to be from a truck tire, or maybe a big van. I'm pretty sure if we find the vehicle, we can get a match."

"A big pickup maybe? Then the shooters would be in the cab, with at least some of our vics riding in the bed."

"Has to be, if this is a print from one of their vehicle's tires."

"Good work, Lurch. I'll see you back at the office. Did you ever find the Dos Equis bottle that goes with the cap?"

"As a matter of fact I did. I'm not sure if it goes with the cap, but it probably does. It smells pretty fresh."

"See if you can get a print off it. We don't have much else to go on."

"You bet."

Tully could see Pap out on the road talking to Harvey Grant, the forest ranger. He walked out and joined them. Most of the other vehicles were pulling out and heading down the road.

Tully said to the ranger, "Harvey, I wish you would patrol these woods a little better and cut down on the murders."

Harvey shook his head. "It's getting almost as bad as the cities. I personally wouldn't go out in the mountains anymore without a weapon. And that's pretty sad, if you ask me. When we were kids, we hiked and camped all over these mountains and never once carried a gun. By the way, I was just telling Pap the FBI is going to be in one hot fuss they weren't notified, this being federal land."

Tully smiled. "Must have slipped my mind. On the other hand, I was up here in the woods all by myself. What's a person to do?"

"You got everybody else alerted. A person can do only so much."

"That's right, Harvey. That'll be my story and I'm sticking to it. Well, I'm sure Pap has been keeping you entertained with accounts of his own murders, but I need him to drive Dave Perkins's vehicle back into town. I'll pick up Dave on my way in."

"You got Dave out doing some tracking for you?" Harvey said.

"Yeah. I think maybe there was a fourth intended victim, and he might have got away. It's a long shot, but if anyone can turn up any sign of him, it'll be Dave."

Harvey smiled. "It's probably that Indian blood. He get his casino started yet?"

Tully rolled his eyes. "Yeah, right, Harvey. Over my dead body."

Pap got in Dave's pickup, whipped it around on the road, and sent rocks flying over the embankment. He headed down the mountain. Tully shook his head, then drove up to a turnout and made a similar maneuver with his own pickup, only much slower.

Then he followed the trail of dust left by Dave's truck. A mile down the mountain he found Pap and Dave standing at the edge of the road. Pap was constructing one of his hand-rolleds. Tully parked on the edge of the road, got out, and walked over to them. "Find anything, Dave?"

"I think your hunch was right, Bo. I did find a few tracks. And a couple of these." He held out a leaf with a spot of dried blood on it.

"That all the blood you found?"

Dave nodded. "There might be more, but there's a lot of brush and I had a hard time staying on his track. He did cut over to the road right here. Stood back behind a tree over there, as if watching for someone." Dave pointed to the tree. "My guess is he was just nicked by the bullet. There's quite a few drops of blood at the base of the tree."

"You think he got a ride with someone?"

"I don't know. He was probably waiting for the shooters to go by. There were signs they had walked down the mountain a ways looking for him but then gave up. Maybe they figured he was hit hard enough he'd die out there in the brush."

Tully walked over and looked at the ground behind the tree. There were faint scuff marks in the pine needles and several tiny dark spots. "You call this 'sign,' Dave — this little disturbance?"

"Yeah, that's what I call it. You want something with his name and address on it? I'm not surprised you don't notice much, Bo, because you have to be Indian to know sign when you see it."

Pap had his cigarette going by now. Tully sighed and stepped upwind of him. "You going back with me, or Dave?"

"Depends on what you're planning to do."

"I'm walking back down that little road we were on until I find some fresh huckleberries. Then I'm going to take a picture of them, if there's still some light. I thought I'd pick enough berries so Ma could make us a couple of pies."

Pap took a drag on his cigarette and blew out a cloud of smoke. "Much as I prefer Dave's company to yours, Bo, the mention of huckleberry pies has caught my attention. I think I'll come along and help you pick."

Pap climbed into Tully's pickup and they drove back up to the old logging road. Tully drove in as far as the downed tree and they got out. "How far we got to walk?" Pap said.

"Only about half a mile from here. You tell anybody about my secret patch, you're a dead man." He handed Pap his extra gallon bucket.

"You got to be kidding me, Bo! A secret patch! About ten thousand people roam about this mountain picking huckleberries every year, and you think you've got a secret patch!"

"Actually, Pap, they don't roam about the mountain. They roam about the roads. There isn't one huckleberry picker in a hundred goes off the road more than fifty feet. If they can't see the road, they think they're lost and start to panic. When you see my secret patch, you're not going to believe it."

"I don't believe it already."

They hiked along in silence for a few minutes. The road had deteriorated into scarcely more than a wide trail. The uphill side, thick with young fir trees, rose steeply up the mountain, and the downhill side dropped off sharply into a heavily logged area. Pap scuffed some dust into the air with his boot. "Dry as a bone out here."

"Yeah, the whole mountain could go up like a box of tinder if we get lightning. If it wasn't so dry, you'd see mushrooms along the road this time of year."

"What kind of mushrooms?"

"Shaggymanes. Giant puffballs."

"I could go for a batch of shaggymanes,"

58

Pap said. "I ain't going to touch another puffball, though. I ate one about five years ago and it nearly killed me."

"I bet it had some yellow in it. It was too old. It has to be pure white all the way through."

"It *was* pure white all the way through! You must think I'm stupid, Bo."

"Then you were drinking."

"A glass of Jack Daniel's before dinner, that's all."

"You should know better than to drink alcohol before eating wild mushrooms! What was that you said about stupid?"

Pap stopped and took a deep breath. "I always drink before dinner, and afterwards, too. I've eaten a ton of wild mushrooms in my life and I never even once before had an attack like that. Anyway, Bo, you picking with your fingers, or did you bring a picker?"

Tully paused and looked down into a drainage dropping sharply below. He had fished the tiny stream years ago. The fish had been small but hungry and plentiful. Back then the trout limit was all you could catch plus one fish. He said, "A picker. I got one for you, too, Pap."

"Good. You buy them from Pinto Jack?"

"Who else? Pinto makes the best huckleberry pickers in the world."

"I have to agree, Bo. I have a whole collection of pickers and not a one comes even close to Pinto's. You know those prongs on the front? He makes them out of bedsprings. They got just the right amount of flex to pop a berry off a bush and not crush it."

They walked along in silence for a ways.

Tully stopped. "This is it."

"What's it? I don't see nothing."

"If everyone could see my secret patch, it wouldn't be secret, would it?" He pointed. "We have to climb up to the ridge there and walk down it a ways."

"There's actually work involved? Now you tell me!"

Tully shook his head. "It's uphill no more than fifty yards. You're always bragging about what good shape you're in, I'm pretty sure you can make fifty yards!"

Pap uttered an expletive. "Of course I can make it! I just like to be warned, that's all. I don't like you sneaking actual work on me without no warning!"

When they reached the top of the ridge, Pap wasn't even breathing hard. Tully once again thought they should put him in ads promoting the use of tobacco and alcohol.

"So where's the secret patch?"

Tully said, "See that little bench going off to our right? We need to hike down it a ways

60

and I'll show you."

Mumbling obscenities, Pap followed Tully down the bench for several dozen yards. "How much farther, Bo?"

"This is it," Tully said.

Pap looked at the huckleberry brush rising almost to his shoulders on both sides of them. He gasped. "I've got to tell you, Bo, I've never seen anything like this!"

Huckleberries the size of grapes hung in huge clusters from the bushes and in some cases dragged the bushes to the ground. The patch stretched all the way down the bench.

"You tell anyone about it, Pap, I'll have to kill you and him."

"Don't worry about me, Bo. I'm amazed the commercial pickers haven't found this and cleaned it out."

"I am too, actually."

Tully hated that there were so many commercial pickers out in the mountains now. They ruined it for everybody else, and some of them were pretty threatening, too, as if they thought you were depriving them of a livelihood by picking a gallon or two. It seemed as if there were more of them every year. He said, "Maybe there are more commercial pickers every year because there are more poor people every year."

"I hate poor people," Pap said. "Most of

your criminals are poor. If we'd do away with poor people we'd do away with most of the crime."

"How about bankers and politicians, Pap? And how about you, speaking of corruption?"

"I may have engaged in a little innocent corruption, but I did it so I wouldn't be one of the poor people I hate."

Tully smiled and shook his head. "I see."

He took out his digital camera and shot close-ups of several clusters of huckleberries. Then he raced Pap to fill his bucket first. Within minutes Pap uttered the classic huckleberry boast: "I've got my bottom covered, Bo!"

"That's one thing I can be thankful for."

Driving down across the meadow to his log house that evening, Tully became aware for the first time how much shorter the days were. It wasn't eight o'clock yet and was already getting dark. He had dropped Pap off at his mansion on the hill and chatted for a while with his gorgeous housekeeper, Deedee, whom Pap had rustled from Dave's House of Fry the previous year. How Deedee put up with the old man, he couldn't fathom, but all signs indicated she was the one in charge. After dropping Pap off and flirting with Deedee, he had driven over to his mother's house and dropped off two gallons of huckleberries. Rose had been thrilled. She tried to talk him into eating something for supper, but Tully was too tired.

When he reached his house he turned the truck off and had a look around his front yard. The grass had all turned brown, probably because his well had dried up. As soon as he had time, he had to dig a new one. He walked in the front door, which he seldom bothered to lock. The large oil painting of his wife greeted him. Ginger had died over ten years before, but the sight of the painting never failed to lift his spirits. He heated a frozen Hungry-Man turkey dinner in the microwave, flipped on the TV, and sat down in his glider to eat and watch a crime show episode he'd seen only twice before. But he had barely begun to eat before he dozed off. The phone rang about twenty minutes later. Reluctantly, he answered. "Sheriff Bo Tully."

"Bo," a man's voice said. "I hope I didn't wake you."

"At this hour? Not a chance."

"This is Pete Reynolds. You told me about the murders up on Scotchman Road earlier today."

"Right, Pete." Tully rubbed his eyes and tried to wake up.

"I talked to some of the drivers about what you said, and George Henderson jumped like he had sat on a hot poker. He said he picked up a young fellow like you mentioned. He come out of the woods and waved George down. He had ripped a sleeve off his shirt and had it wrapped around his upper right arm. George asked him how he hurt it, and he said he'd fallen on a log and jabbed it with a broken limb. He was kind of pale and George said he would be glad to drive him by the hospital and drop him off at the emergency room, but the kid wouldn't have nothing to do with that. When they got down to Blight City, he said he would be fine, so George pulled over and stopped. The kid thanked him and got out, and that's the last George seen of him."

"Pete, this is wonderful! I find that kid, I've got the shooters. Did George say exactly where in Blight he dropped him off?"

"Yeah, right after you cross the railroad tracks when you come into town from the Scotchman Road."

"You did great, Pete! I owe you one!"

"I hope that means if logging don't pick up, you'll add me to the force."

"I've hired a lot worse, I can tell you that. You may have helped blow this case wide open, Pete. Many thanks."

He sat back down in his glider to finish eating. No way he would ever get back to sleep now.

7

Tully woke up at seven with *Good Morning America* on the TV and the Hungry-Man turkey dinner half-eaten and cold in his lap. One of these days he meant to get a life.

On his way into the office, Tully stopped at McDonald's for coffee and an Egg McMuffin, his third one for breakfast that week. By the time he walked into the briefing room, the day shift had already gone out. He stuck his head in the radio room and said, "Morning, Flo." She treated him to one of the smiles she seemed to reserve only for him.

Daisy was typing up something on her computer and Herb was reading the morning paper. As expected, Lurch was hard at work in his corner. Tully yelled at him, "Hey, Lurch!"

"Morning, boss!"

Tully walked over. "You get any prints off that beer bottle?"

"Yeah, got a match, too."

"No kidding. Anyone we know?"

"Lennie Frick."

Tully frowned. "Frick? He did a couple of months for multiple DUIs, and before that — what was it, Lurch?"

"Theft of a roll of telephone wire off a utility company truck. Sold it for the copper."

"Right. I can't imagine Lennie moving up to triple murder. So what's his current address?"

"You expect me to know everything, boss?"

"Yeah. What is it?"

"It's Four-oh-five East Sharp."

"I'll swing by and have a little visit with him. Thanks, Lurch."

"You bet." Lurch went back to his computer.

Tully walked across the briefing room. Daisy pretended she was too busy to notice his approach.

"Bring your pad, sweetheart."

Daisy sighed loudly but then got up and followed him into his office. Tully stood by the door and closed it behind her.

She sat down in a chair across from his desk, her back straight, her knees crossed below the short black skirt, and said, "I

67

already have a ton of work to get done this morning, Bo. I hope you don't have a ton more."

"No, I don't, Daisy. I was just wondering how you're getting along these days."

"Where are we going with this?"

Tully smiled. "Nowhere. It's just been a while since I talked to you. All I want to know is if you're okay."

Daisy squinted at him. "Yeah, I'm okay."

"Good, because I've got some more work for you."

"I thought so."

"Get on the phone and your computer and find out everything you can about Lennie Frick. Known associates, possession of firearms, and things like that. I need it all about an hour ago."

Daisy shook her head and laughed. "You're something else, boss, you know that?"

"I suppose. You know, Daisy, you're not only the best deputy I've got, you're also the prettiest by far."

"I'm not up to that again."

"I suppose. Forget I mentioned it."

Daisy smiled. "But thanks anyway, Bo." She went out and closed the door behind her.

Tully picked up the phone and dialed. His

mother answered. "I knew it would be you, Bo."

"Just wanted to say good morning, Ma."

"I'm sure. The answer is, yes, I already have four huckleberry pies in the oven. One each for you and Pap, and two for me. I carved a *B* in the crust of yours, and be sure you eat that one. I put arsenic in Pap's."

"I think that's a crime, Ma, but it's okay, as long as you marked the right one. I'll swing by later and pick them up."

He hung up and drummed his fingers on the desk while he thought about what to do next. Too bad he had given up smoking his pipe, because that would give him something to do while he thought. He got up and walked out to Daisy's desk. "Do you know where Pugh is?"

"He's on his way in. Brian worked until after midnight yesterday."

"I suppose he thinks that's an excuse for coming late to work."

"Yeah, he's such a slacker."

"Send him in as soon as he gets here."

"Yes, sir, boss."

He walked back to his office and stood for a moment staring out the window at Lake Blight. Only he could no longer see the lake because the window had been painted over. One of his criminals had taken a shot at

69

him from a boat and missed him and Daisy by half an inch. Daisy had saved his life at the risk of her own. That had led to the brief affair. Hard to tell what other catastrophe might occur if another nut took a shot at him from the lake. So he'd had the window painted over.

Deputy Brian Pugh stuck his head in the door. "You want to see me, boss?" He was carrying a cup of coffee.

"Yeah, Pugh. Come in and grab a chair. What have you been up to?"

"Ernie and I were out last night trying to shake down some guys for info about that rumored marijuana stash." He grabbed a chair with one hand, spun it around, and sat down astraddle it across from Tully. Although Pugh was still in his thirties, Tully was pleased to see he was already picking up a bit of gray in his hair. The deputy shoved some papers aside and set his cup on Tully's desk. Pugh, Ernie Thorpe, and Daisy were his only plainclothes deputies.

"Get anything?"

"Not much. I've never seen so many bad guys tight-lipped about somebody else's deal, if it *is* somebody else's deal. They knew we could do them some favors, too, and maybe some hurt, but they wouldn't give us zip. I think they were scared."

"Really?"

"Yeah, really. You know our bad guys are pussycats compared with what's running around in the big cities."

Tully tugged on the corner of his mustache and thought about this. "What you're telling me, Brian, is that maybe some really heavy dudes have moved into town?"

"That's the feeling both Ernie and I get. Usually we don't have any trouble shaking loose a few tidbits of info, but now we're getting nothing. We even offered to drop some possession charges, but still nothing."

"You're right, our criminals usually don't refuse a deal."

Pugh took a sip of his coffee and made a face. "Where does Daisy get this stuff anyway?"

"Straight from China, at fifteen cents a pound. So don't be picky. You think the three dead guys I found up in the huckleberry patch yesterday might have something to do with it?"

"The coffee? Yeah, they were probably the importers. Serves them right."

"No, the fact you can't pry any info out of your snitches."

Pugh nodded. "That did occur to me. But why would they kill three huckleberry pickers?"

"Maybe the pickers had stumbled onto somebody's secret patch. Who knows? Actually, there were four intended victims. The fourth one got away. I think he was nicked in the arm by one of the shooters. Dave tracked him down the mountain for a mile and only found a few spots of blood. So he couldn't have been hit hard. Brian, I want you to drop everything else and find this guy. I'm pretty sure he will know who the shooters are."

Pugh stood up and retrieved his coffee cup. "You're probably right about that. You got any idea where I can find this picker?"

"George Henderson gave the kid a ride off the mountain in his logging truck and dropped him off just across the tracks where the Scotchman Peak Road comes into Blight. You know George?"

"The logger? Sure, I know who he is."

"Good. George should be able to give you a description of the guy. The kid probably isn't over twenty and hasn't had a shower in a few months. I checked the hands on the dead victims and they were all rough and callused, like they were farmworkers. So this guy probably resembles the other vics, but a little smarter."

Pugh smiled. "A dirty, young, smart farmworker. Shouldn't take me any time at all to find him."

"Don't be a wise guy, Pugh. The fact that the other vics hadn't come in contact with bathwater in a year probably applies to him, too. Even if he was only slightly nicked by a bullet, the wound would get infected. If it does, he'll probably show up at the hospital emergency room to get it treated. The kid isn't stupid. Otherwise, he'd be dead."

Pugh stood up to leave. "I know a nurse who works emergency. I'll check with her."

"The cute redhead?"

"How did you know, boss?"

"Maybe I'm psychic."

Pugh laughed. "Yeah, I bet. I've got my eye on her myself. Any other leads on the shooters?"

"Lennie Frick."

"Frick! You've got to be kidding me, Bo! If Frick went to swat a fly, the fly would take the swatter away and beat him with it!"

Tully shrugged. "But who knows what evil dwells in the heart of any man?"

"Hunh? I think you need to take a few days off, boss."

"You're probably right, Pugh. I need to relax a little. As a matter of fact, I'm thinking of phoning a beautiful fortune-teller and inviting her to lunch."

Pugh shook his head. "I'm not kidding, boss. You need some time off!"

8

Tully drove over to 405 East Sharp. It was a tiny, ratty-looking house, scarcely big enough for the rats, let alone Frick. Parked out front was a battered red pickup truck with a blue door, the door no doubt salvaged at night from a wrecking yard. In the front of the house was a pile of empty beer cans taller than Tully. It appeared as if each can was the same brand of beer, Acme, the worst beer he had ever tasted but also the cheapest. He knocked on the front door. A voice inside called out, "Who is it?"

"The police, Frick. And don't try running out the back, because I've got men out there who will beat you senseless for the fun of it!"

The door opened a crack and Frick peeked out. "Oh, it's only you, Bo." He unhooked a chain and opened the door the rest of the way. "Come on in."

Tully preferred his criminals to have more

fear of him. "No, Lennie, you come out."

Frick stepped out. He was wearing a dirty T-shirt, grungy jeans, and a pair of wire-rim glasses taped together over the nosepiece. His hair appeared to have been cut with a lawn mower. He nodded at the pile of beer cans. "What do you think of my collection, Bo?"

"Very nice, Lennie. All the same make of beer, I see."

"Yeah. I'm kind of a perfectionist. Me and my buddies emptied them all ourselves. I wouldn't let anybody toss on anything but an Acme can."

"I can see that. But occasionally you treat yourself to a Dos Equis, don't you, Lennie?"

"Jeez, how'd you know that?"

"Because we found a Dos Equis bottle at a crime scene and it had your prints on it."

Lennie looked as if he was about to faint. "I-I-I didn't do nothing to nobody, Bo!"

Tully smiled. "I know you didn't, Lennie. But if you tell me one itty-bitty lie, you're going to jail for it. Now, when you were up on that old logging road on the Scotchman, did you see anything unusual?"

Lennie was silent. Tully could almost hear the brain cells grinding together as he sorted through all the petty crimes he had committed in the last week. "No, nothing. There's a huckleberry patch in there a ways, pretty well picked over, and I got a gallon for my mom."

"Good for her. Did you notice anything unusual about the huckleberry patch?"

"Like what?"

"Three dead bodies."

Lennie's jaw dropped. "No! I didn't see no bodies!"

Tully tugged on the corner of his mustache as he stared coldly at the perfectionist. "Okay, I believe you, Lennie. Now tell me exactly when you were up there."

Lennie frowned. Tully could see his fingers down along his side, counting. "Three days ago."

"You're sure?"

"Yeah. I dropped the berries off at my mom's and she baked me a pie. I picked the pie up yesterday."

"So what time did you drive back down from Scotchman?"

"Jeez, it was pretty late. Maybe about four. Still mighty hot, though."

"Did you see anybody when you were driving back down the road? Any other pickers, for example?"

"Naw. Oh, there was one big white pickup parked at a turnout on the road when I was

77

coming down. It had a bunch of young guys sitting in the bed. The pickup looked brand-new."

"Anything unusual about it?"

"Yeah, it was one of them dualies. That's the kind of pickup I'm going to buy next."

"You're saying it had dual tires on the rear, right?"

"Right."

"Anything else unusual about it?"

"Only the folks inside. A bunch of stuck-up rich guys. I waved when I drove by but not a one of them waved back. Then it occurred to me maybe they were having car trouble. So I stopped and backed up. The driver rolled down his window and I asked him if he needed any help. He said, 'Beat it!' and called me a nasty name. I would have said something back just as rude but he didn't seem like the kind of person you want to be rude to. So I just drove on."

"You think you could pick that guy out of a lineup?"

"Yeah, I'll never forget that face."

Tully gave Lennie his cold stare again. "Now, listen to me very closely. First, get in that red truck of yours with the blue door and park it in that little garage you've got out back. Don't drive it anywhere, until you hear from me."

"You're scaring me, Bo."

"I intend to. Now, do you remember how many people were in the cab?"

"Yeah, there was three of them, all in the front seat. The backseat was empty. It was still blistering hot out, and they had these other guys riding in the bed. All four of them could have fit into the backseat. You can bet the cab was air-conditioned."

Tully smiled. "You've done good. Just remember now, for once in your life, Lennie, you can't be dumb. Let me repeat, you can't be dumb! Don't drive that pickup anywhere until you get that blue door replaced and until you hear from me."

"How come, Bo?"

"Because somebody will kill you, Lennie, that's why."

9

Back at the courthouse, Tully walked directly into his office. He thumbed through his phone book. No luck. He punched a button on his phone and got Daisy's extension.

"Yeah, boss."

"Daisy, work some of your magic and find Etta Gorsich's number for me."

"Why? You need your fortune told?"

"No! Just get me her number!"

A few minutes later Daisy came in and handed him the number on a piece of paper.

"That was fast. It's not in the book. Where did you find it?"

"I called your mom."

"Ma had it?"

"Of course. She keeps track of all the gossip, in this world and the next."

"I should have known." He hung up and dialed the number. Etta Gorsich answered.

"Etta, it's Bo Tully."

"Bo! So good to hear from you! I would love to!"

"Uh, how do you know what I have in mind?"

"Whatever it is, Bo, I would love to."

"Well, that's, uh, great. What I have in mind is lunch at Crabbs. Can I meet you there in an hour?"

"Perfect. See you there in an hour, Bo."

Scarcely had he hung up the phone when Daisy buzzed him. "Marge Poulson is headed your way. Are you in?"

"Daisy, how can I not be in? This office has glass on three sides."

"Last time you hid under your desk."

"I'll see her! Show her in."

He walked over and opened the door for Mrs. Poulson. She was in her early sixties, a few years younger than her ex-husband, Orville. She was one stern lady, a ranchwoman who had grown up in hard times, and all nonsense had long ago been washed out of her. She came directly to the point.

"Sheriff, when are you going to arrest Ray Crockett for the murder of Orville?"

"Would you like to sit down?" he asked, pointing to the chair in front of his desk.

"No, I simply want you to answer my question."

"As I've told you before, Mrs. Poulson,

we have no evidence that Orville is even dead. We obviously can't arrest someone simply on your suspicions."

Her shoulders seemed to slump.

"Please sit down," he said, putting his arm around her and edging her toward the chair. She sat. Tully walked around his desk and sat down across from her.

The woman seemed tired and a little dazed, but something caught her attention. "Why is that window painted over, Sheriff?"

Tully turned and glanced at the window. Good question. "Well, one of our local criminals tried to shoot me through it a while back."

"Oh, yes, I read about that in the paper. I'm sorry, Sheriff, I know you have lots of problems, and I shouldn't be such a bother, but the murder of Orville weighs on me something awful. We have been divorced for five years but we were married for nearly forty. I don't know about other people, but just because Orville and I couldn't stand living with each other anymore doesn't mean we stopped caring. I know your wife died ten years ago, Sheriff, and you've never married again. You understand about attachment."

Her words caught Tully off guard. He felt a sudden constriction in his throat and hoped his eyes hadn't teared up. "Yes, I do, Marge." He cleared his throat. "I want you to know I haven't for a minute forgotten about Orville. What I'm about to tell you is between the two of us. If you breathe a word of it to anyone, it could get me in a lot of trouble and we might never find out what happened to your husband. So give me your word."

"You have it, Sheriff."

"I went out and met Ray Crockett the other day. He's a pretty smooth customer and seems like a pleasant enough fellow. Nevertheless, I suspect he did Orville in, just as you suspect. More likely, he had somebody else do it. But we have to find the body. And a body can be hard to find if the person isn't even dead."

Marge took out a hanky and dabbed at her eyes. "Oh, Orville could be buried anywhere out there. That ranch is over a thousand acres. Do you even have a clue where he might be?"

Tully didn't want to tell her he had a lead, because he didn't even know if he had one. "No, I don't," he said. "Crockett told me he mails Orville's Social Security checks to a post office box in Spokane each month. If, in fact, Orville has been murdered by him, Crockett must then go to Spokane, pick up the checks, and cash them. I'm not sure how difficult it is for someone to cash Social Security checks belonging to someone else. By the way, Marge, are you having any financial problems because of Orville's disappearance?"

She laughed. "You don't have to worry about me, Sheriff. I'm well off. Orville gave me half the money from his sale of the stock. Then I rented out the old farmhouse I inherited from my folks. The renters don't farm but say they like the isolation. There aren't any neighbors within miles."

"Where's the farmhouse?"

"It's a few miles down the road from my own little house, on the other side of Cow Creek. As for cashing Social Security checks belonging to someone else, I have no idea." Marge put her hanky back in her purse. "His Social Security checks didn't amount to that much."

"How much?"

"About fifteen hundred dollars. Not enough for somebody to murder a person for."

"Marge, people get murdered for a whole lot less than fifteen hundred dollars. Take my word for it."

"Really? It seems so little for a human life."

"Yes, it does. I guess the value goes down pretty fast if it's somebody else's life. In any case, Marge, I'll get in touch with you as soon as I know something."

"Thanks, Bo. Is it okay if I call you Bo?"

"You bet. You can call me anything you like, Marge. Oh, I understand Orville was quite the fisherman."

"Good heavens, no! Orville hated fishing. Said it was the most boring excuse for a hobby he could ever imagine. Why do you ask?"

"No reason. Just something I heard."

10

After Marge left, Tully drove over to Crabbs. Etta was just getting out of her car when he arrived. She was dressed in what, to Tully, looked like sailcloth pants, the legs spreading into little flares slightly below her calves. She wore a little black jacket that also seemed to have an ancient naval look to it, although maybe it was just basic New Yorky, something she had picked up at Saks Fifth Avenue. Ever since Susan, he had made a point of being attentive to what women wore.

"Hey, Bo!" Etta cried. "We have perfect timing!"

As with almost everything Etta said, Tully wondered if there weren't something subliminal he was supposed to pick up on. He had never known a woman who made him quite as nervous as this one. Having enough trouble with his present world, he had little tolerance for people who claimed a knowledge of some other world. He hoped Etta wasn't one of those. She had impressed him as a person of few pretensions. The outside of her house displayed only cracked and peeling paint, a rickety porch, a yard that made Lennie Frick's beer-can pile look like a landscaper's display piece, and a set of stairs and handrails in serious need of warning signs. If she ran a business out of her house, she needed a visit from OSHA. Now he noticed that she drove a rather modest Buick LeSabre with several dents and dings, and in need of a wash. On the other hand, everything in the interior of her house had been strictly upscale. Something weird was going on with Etta Gorsich.

"Hey, Etta!" he called back.

She gave him one of her sexy but amused smiles. "I hope I'm not taking you away from your work."

"Actually, you are," he said. "And I'm profoundly grateful."

Etta responded with a throaty laugh. "I'm pleased, then. I've never dated a sheriff before. But maybe this isn't a date. Maybe it's only a business lunch."

"I prefer to think of it as a date," Tully said. "Crabbs, by the way, is the best restaurant in all of Blight City."

Etta smiled. "Sad, isn't it?"

"Yes, it is. Its strongest point is proximity. Crabbs's motto should be 'We're here.' "

"Perfect!" she said. "You should be in advertising, Bo."

"You really think so?"

"No, I think you're perfect as the sheriff. People love you, particularly the women."

Tully took her by the arm and turned her, so he could look her in the eye. "You've been talking to my mother, haven't you, Etta?"

"Your mother? Good heavens, no!"

"Come clean. I'm a sheriff, you know. I can spot a lie three blocks away."

She put on an exaggerated pout. "Well, if your mother is a fascinating woman named Rose, it's entirely possible I may have met her on some occasion."

Tully rolled his eyes. "Just as I thought! My mother is Gossip Central in Blight City and surrounding points. I happen to be the main topic of her gossip. You should never believe a single thing she says."

Etta pretended to be extremely serious. "But isn't it true, Bo, that all the women love you?"

"Well, that's true, of course. I mean all the other stuff."

"I'll say only this about my conversations

with Rose: the other stuff is extremely interesting!"

Tully let his chin drop down onto his
chest.

Lester Cline, the manager, showed them
to a table. Tully watched as he spread a
napkin on Etta's lap. She ran her eyes down
the menu.

She looked up. "I'd love to go with the
beef dip but I'm afraid I'd drip the *jus* all
over me."

"You obviously have sophisticated tastes,
Etta. I usually order the beef dip myself."
He nodded at the manager.

"Yes, sir?" Lester said. "The usual?"

"One for each of us, please."

Lester hurried off. Etta leaned across the
table toward Tully. "Didn't you just hear me
say I was afraid I'd drip *jus* all over me?"

"I did, indeed. Ah, here comes Lester."

"Already?"

Lester came up behind Etta and tied a
plastic bib around her neck. It went all the
way down her front and covered her lap.
For a moment, she seemed shocked. Then
she burst out in a raucous laugh, much to
Tully's relief. Lester then tied a bib around
Tully's neck. Etta now laughed so hard she
seemed in pain.

Lester took a pad from his pocket. "And

what dressing would you like on your salads?"

Etta appeared incapable of speech. "Blue cheese on both, Lester," Tully said.

He tried to steer their conversation over lunch in a sensible direction. Etta was eating the beef dip with appropriate gusto and had an attentive expression on her face. Then suddenly she exploded with wild laughter, holding her napkin in front of her face, struggling to maintain a certain propriety.

"Am I correct to assume you don't usually wear bibs at your New York restaurants?" Tully asked.

Etta stretched the napkin like a curtain in front of her face. Her eyes peered over the top, full of tears and pain. She shook her head slowly back and forth — then broke out laughing again.

By the time the waiter took away their bibs and plates and returned with cups of coffee and a small plate of chocolates, Etta looked as if she were headed out for trick-or-treating. Streaks of mascara ran down both cheeks, but she had finally settled into an enduring calm.

"I hope you're sorry," she said.

"I can't believe you've never used a bib before."

"Not since I was about four years old. And don't you dare set me off again. The other customers in here probably think I'm crazed."

Tully held up his hands as if claiming total innocence. "I'm sorry. I had no idea a bib would have such an effect. In any case, I have an important question I need to ask you, in all seriousness."

"You're sure?"

"Yes. When I left your place the other day, you called after me from your porch, 'Look under the house.' What did you mean?"

Etta frowned. "I didn't call after you, 'Look under the house.' At least I certainly don't remember doing so. Why would I say something like that? I've never even seen your house."

"Not my house. Somebody else's house."

"Somebody else's house? I don't know what you're talking about, Bo."

Tully shook his head. "Here's the thing, Etta. It seemed to refer to a case I've been working on."

"Bo, I know nothing about your cases. If I were actually a psychic, I probably could solve all your cases for you, but I'm not. My expertise is financial counseling. I can

91

assure you I didn't call out anything to you."

"Forget I asked. Please! It was stupid of me."

Etta turned sober. "I will tell you something, Bo. I really don't have answers to anything. I'm not a psychic. Not a fortune-teller. I barely know what I'll be doing from one day to the next, let alone managing to predict the future for someone else. But occasionally an odd image will flash in my mind for no reason at all. Maybe I did blurt something out. If I did, it meant absolutely nothing."

Tully didn't know what to say or do. "Etta, it isn't important. I'm sorry I brought it up."

"I hope I haven't ruined our lunch, Bo. By the way, please tell me this really is a date. I'm badly in need of a date."

"Me too. It's definitely a date, Etta. I hope we can have another one soon."

"You don't think I'm weird, Bo?"

"Well, yeah."

It was a test. Etta passed. She laughed.

11

Tully got back to the office in early afternoon. Lurch called to him as he came in. "Hey, boss, Susan says she's recovered three bullets from the vics. All three are .22-caliber shorts. I've got a theory about that."

"Let's hear it."

"I think the shooters used silencers."

"What makes you think that?"

"The fact the bullets were .22-caliber shorts. You want to kill somebody dead, you don't use .22 shorts. You're trying to hold the sound down. You want to really hold it down, you use silencers."

Tully scratched his head. "Interesting theory, Lurch. If the shooters used silencers, we're dealing with serious criminals. Our local boys wouldn't know a silencer from a bass drum. Susan sending the bullets over?"

"I told her I'd pick them up."

"Good. Too bad silencers don't leave

marks. We may turn some up, though. Did you get the prints on the vics?"

"Yeah, but no matches, boss."

Tully headed back to his office. "Weird. I was hoping we might at least get a lead."

He stopped at Daisy's desk. Without looking up she said, "I know this can't be good. Besides, I smell a woman."

"You must be psychic."

"So, how was lunch with Etta Gorsich?"

"Not bad. Couldn't hold a candle to lunch with you, though."

Daisy checked her notepad. "I bet not. But to get back to business, Brian called. Said he wants you to meet him at three at Slade's Bar and Grill."

"Pugh say why?"

"He said it had to do with the killings up on Scotchman."

Tully frowned. "Slade's is in a rough part of town."

"Criminals seem fond of the place. Actually, he said to meet him across the street from Slade's."

"Probably wants me to watch his backside."

Daisy smiled. "I think the expression is 'watch his back.' "

"Is that it? I'm always getting my cop expressions mixed up."

■ ■ ■ ■

Pugh was sitting in his blue Ford pickup across the street from Slade's. Tully drove up behind him in an unmarked department car. He walked up and climbed into the passenger seat of Pugh's truck. "What's the plan, Brian?"

"There's a hooker works out of here. Some guy beat her up pretty bad the other night. A small-time hood by the name of Jack Foley hangs out at Slade's. Deals some drugs and has a two-bit fencing operation. I could have busted him half a dozen times, but a year in jail would seem like a resort vacation to him. He tells me there are three very serious dudes in town. Been hanging out here all summer. The other night one of them cracked Bev — that's the hooker — up alongside the head with a pistol. Rang her bell pretty bad. The three guys have been sitting at her table about every evening they come in. I suspect Bev spouted out something she shouldn't have, probably something she heard from one of them."

Tully tugged thoughtfully on the corner of his mustache. "So, what do you need me for, Brian? This looks like a place I could get seriously hurt."

"Yeah, it is, boss. I thought you might like to come along to keep me from killing some of the patrons."

"I see. Well, I suppose I could do that."

They got out of the pickup and walked across the street. Tully pulled his Stetson low over his eyes and peered into the darkened interior. He could make out half a dozen figures moving around in the back. He and Pugh walked in and sat down at the bar. The bartender approached, eyeing them suspiciously.

"Two double shots of whiskey," Tully said.

Pugh gave Tully a look.

Tully winked at him. "Might as well enjoy this, Brian. Besides, I need something to settle my nerves."

The bartender brought their drinks. "Listen, fellas," he said in a low voice. "The guys here usually don't care for strangers dropping by. Be a good idea to finish your drinks and clear out."

Tully leaned across the bar and whispered, "We're actually pretty tough. Particularly my partner here. Sometimes I have to restrain him, keep him from going too far, you know what I mean?"

The bartender shrugged. "Just giving you some free advice."

Tully glanced at the group playing pool at

the far end of the room. "It's Friday afternoon," he said. "Doesn't anyone in here have a regular job?"

"Yeah," the bartender said. "Me."

"Is Bev around?" Pugh asked.

"Yeah, she's sitting at the table over in the corner. She isn't feeling so good. A fella gave her a pretty rough time the other night and she's closed for business. Her, uh, boyfriend is that big guy shooting pool in the back with the guys. It's always a good idea to talk to him first, before you talk to Bev."

"Really," Tully said. "Well, we don't usually ask permission to talk to anybody, right, Bud?"

Pugh was studying the big guy.

"Bud!" Tully said, nudging Pugh in the ribs.

"Oh, yeah, right."

They picked up their drinks and walked over to Bev's table. She was holding an ice bag against the side of her head. As Pap might have said, she looked rode hard and put away wet.

She peered up at them with the eye that wasn't swollen shut. "I'm out of commission, guys."

Tully pulled out a chair and sat down. Pugh took the chair next to him. Tully said,

"We need to talk to you, Bev, about the guy who smacked you with the pistol."

"You better talk fast, then," she said, "because here comes J.D."

A second later the huge man was looming over them. Tully and Pugh looked up at him.

The monster said, "I guess you guys don't know the rules, so I'll tell you. Clear out now, before I throw you out."

"I'm sorry, sir," Tully said, "but we were talking to the young lady."

"You ain't talking to nobody! Now out!"

Tully smiled at Pugh. "Your turn or my turn?"

"I think it's yours. I've had the last dozen. But I'll take it, boss. Hospital?"

"A couple days would be about right."

Pugh stood up. He stuck his head out around J.D. and yelled at the bartender. "You better call an ambulance. I think my friend here is having an attack of some kind."

The bartender stared at him. Then Tully heard two quick thumps. J.D. groaned and crumpled to the floor.

"Don't just stand there," Pugh yelled at the bartender. "This man is having an attack of some kind. Get an ambulance."

The bartender snatched up a phone and dialed.

Bev blinked her good eye. "Who are you guys, anyway?"

Tully wanted to say, I'm the masked man and this is my loyal sidekick, Tonto. Instead he said, "I'm Blight County sheriff Bo Tully, and this is my deputy Brian Pugh. I could arrest you if I wanted to, Bev, but instead I'm going to put you under protective custody. We need to know everything you can remember about that guy who hit you the other night."

She lifted the ice bag from the bruised side of her face. "It was one of the three guys come in here two, three times a week. I said something smart to the jerk and, wham, he hits me. Knocked me right out of my chair. I woke up on the floor. When I came to, they were gone. Joey said J.D. didn't lift a finger. I guess everybody was scared to death of them."

"And Joey is . . . ?" Pugh said.

She pointed with the ice bag. "He's the bartender. You can ask Joey about those guys, but he won't tell you nothing. He's as scared of them as everybody else."

Tully looked over at the bartender. "I think maybe he'll talk to me, Bev. Right now Brian here is going to take you to a hospital and have you checked out. Then he'll find you a place to stay. He'll get you everything you need. You don't have to worry. No one is going to hurt you anymore. I'll talk to you tomorrow."

The ambulance arrived so quickly Tully thought it must have been in the neighborhood. The medics wheeled in a stretcher, rolled J.D. onto it, and hauled him out. The big man was groaning and holding his side. Pugh helped Bev to his truck. Tully walked over to talk to the bartender. He showed him his badge.

"Joey, do you know if J.D. ever had an attack like that before?"

"I don't think so. Not that I know of, anyway."

"You might want to search your memory."

"Uh, yeah, now that you mention it, I think maybe."

"Good. Now, I want you to tell me everything you know about the guy who hit Bev."

"Gee, I don't know nothing about him. I'm the wrong person to ask."

Tully smiled. "It wasn't a request, Joey. I want you to tell me every last bit of information you have about that fellow and his two friends. If you're afraid of them, let me tell you, Joey, you're afraid of the wrong people."

"Okay, okay, I'll tell you what I know. It ain't that much. Him and his two friends

100

have been hanging out here all summer. Actually, I think they first showed up sometime in the spring. They come in two, three times a week. The one hit Bev is the nice one of the three. The other two are stone cold. I can't even describe them."

"They been here today?"

"No, they haven't been back since the guy hit Bev. I hope they don't come back. The other two seemed pretty upset with the one that hit her. I don't think they like that kind of attention."

"You say they've been coming here since last spring?"

"Yeah. Maybe about the beginning of May. They never caused no trouble before. They just sat and drank and talked to Bev. Even so, they scared people. I bet our business dropped by half after they started hanging out here."

Tully handed the bartender his card. "If any of them show up here again, Joey, give me a call."

Joey looked at the card. "Sure."

"Let me explain once again, Joey. I'm not making a request."

"Right, Sheriff. They show up, I'll give you a call."

For the first time, Tully noticed a strange silence in the bar. He looked toward the back. All the pool players were standing there, staring at him. "Go back to your game, boys," he called. "The entertainment is over."

12

Tully dropped off his unmarked car in the Sheriff's Department's garage and went up to the office. Daisy had cleaned off her desk and was getting ready to leave.

"Any word from Pugh?" he asked.

"Yeah, he called from the hospital. He said the guy who had the attack at Slade's apparently had a kidney problem. They're going to run some tests."

"Good. I hope they're all painful. Anything else?"

"Yes, come to think of it. Your fortune-teller called and asked that you get in touch."

Tully grimaced. "First of all, Daisy, Etta Gorsich is not a fortune-teller. Second, she isn't mine."

"If you say so, boss."

Tully stood there and glared as Daisy picked up her purse and strode out the door, her high heels clicking smartly on the

103

marble-chip floor. Then he shrugged. By Monday he would be able to think up a good response. He would call Etta tomorrow.

He gulped down a hamburger and a beer in Crabbs Lounge and then drove over to the hospital. The cute redheaded nurse was working the admissions desk, but there was a line of people waiting for her attention. He sat down in the waiting room to give the line time to shorten. A drunk was at that moment pleading for her attention. She frowned sternly at him and pointed toward the waiting room. Tully grabbed up a magazine and pretended to read. He knew the drunk would head directly for him. He was a magnet for drunks. The guy sat down beside him. He looked and smelled as if he had been living in a Dumpster for the past month.

"I got beat up," he told Tully.

"That right?" Tully didn't look up from his magazine. He noticed he was staring at an ad on the latest weight-loss miracle.

"Yeah," the drunk said. "My brother did it."

"Oh."

"Yeah, my own brother. Can you believe that?"

Tully detected that the fellow hadn't been

near bathwater in perhaps a year. He thought maybe his eyes were starting to water, because the weight-loss ad had blurred. He lowered the magazine and looked over at the nurse. A city cop was talking to her. The redhead pointed at the drunk. The cop turned and looked. He was a big guy, with a nose that had been broken too many times and multiple scars scattered about his face. His name was Tim Doyle and he worked the neighborhood that surrounded Slade's. He walked over and said hello to Tully. Then he spoke to the drunk. "You're coming with me, Willy."

"How come, Tim?" Willy said. "I didn't do nothing."

"You called in a complaint that Lyle assaulted you. Now I want you to come with me to hunt down Lyle. You make a complaint, we have to follow up on it."

"Okay." The drunk pushed himself up out of the chair.

Relieved, Tully lowered his magazine. "How's it going, Tim?"

"Same ol', same ol', Bo. Bet you're here to check out Scarlett."

"If by any chance you mean that lovely redheaded nurse over there, Tim, nothing could be further from my mind. What I really like is to stop by for conversations

105

with people like Willy here."

"I bet. Well, Willy's all right. Come on, Willy."

Tully watched them. As the cop and Willy walked by the admissions desk, Scarlett called out, "Take care of yourself, Willy! You too, Tim!"

Willy beamed at her.

Tim shook his head. "He's going to be riding around with me the rest of the night, Scarlett."

The admittance line had disappeared for the moment. Tully got up and walked over. Odd, he thought. They're like some strange underground family here, cop, nurse, drunk, people who see one another almost every day. It's as if they look out for one another.

Scarlett glanced up. "You have to be Sheriff Bo Tully. I'm Scarlett O'Ryan. I've heard a lot about you."

"From whom, may I ask?"

"Your deputies, of course. They come in here to get patched up."

"I'm not surprised. They're a careless bunch. So you're the famous redhead. I can see now the boys haven't been exaggerating."

She laughed. "They're pretty nice boys, Sheriff."

"Call me Bo, please. Everybody does, even

my criminals."

"I hear you're quite the fly fisherman, Bo."

Tully nodded. "Yeah, but I'm mostly a catch-and-eat kind of guy. Wet a fly now and then. That way I don't catch so many fish it becomes a distraction. I know some great fly-fishing streams, by the way, if you're interested in taking up the sport."

"Is that an invitation, Bo?"

"It definitely is. I'd be most happy to give you a few lessons."

She laughed. "Really? My father started me out with a fly rod when I was eight years old, if those are the kind of lessons you had in mind."

"They most certainly are. You probably can give me some lessons, Scarlett. Let's see, my mind seems to have gone blank for a second. Oh, yeah, I was going to say that right at the moment I'm tied up with some crimes and stuff like that. But I should be free in a couple of weeks. I'll, uh, be in touch. But back to business. You may have had a kid about twenty come in here to get a wound in his arm treated. Would have been the last few days."

"Sure, I remember him. I helped patch him up. He said he had fallen on a sharp stick but both the doctor and I thought it was a bullet wound. We cleaned it up, put in a couple stitches, and gave him a shot of penicillin."

"He give you a name and address?"

She shook her head. "He did but they were both obviously fake. He didn't have any ID on him. Called himself something like Bill Brown. I can look up the name and address for you if you want."

"Naw. They'd both be phony. Maybe if the wound gets infected he'll come in again. Give me a call, will you?"

"Sure."

"One other thing, Scarlett. My deputy Brian Pugh . . ."

"I know Brian."

"Of course you do. He was supposed to bring in a not-so-young lady earlier. Is he still here by any chance?"

"I haven't seen him leave. Hold on a sec, I'll check." She punched a couple of buttons and spoke into a speaker. "Is Brian still back there?"

Brian? Tully thought. So he's that well known around here.

"Yeah," a voice said. "Who wants him?"

"His boss. At emergency reception."

"He's on his way."

Brian came striding out. "So you tracked me down, Bo. What's up?"

"I was just checking on our two patients."

"They're going to keep Bev a couple of days for observation. She was hurt a lot worse than anybody at Slade's knew or let on. She'll be all right, though. J.D. apparently had a bruised kidney or something like that. Probably got it from a fall. But he should be out tomorrow."

"Good. J.D. will probably be politer to strangers in the future."

"I suspect so."

Brian nodded at the nurse. "I see you've met Scarlett."

"Bo and I may go fishing together in a couple of weeks," she said.

Pugh laughed. "I told you he works fast."

"Actually, Brian, I think I was the one who worked fast."

Scarlett was about to add something when her phone rang. She picked it up and said, "Blight City Emergency." She listened. "Yeah, Tim, he's still here."

She handed the phone to Tully. "Tim Doyle."

Tully took the phone. "Hi, Tim. What's up?"

"Bo, we just had a shooting outside the K-Bar convenience store on the north side. I think it's something you might be interested in. I'm on my way there. You want to swing by?"

"I'll be there in fifteen minutes, Tim. Thanks for the call."

Scarlet looked up at him. "Business, I bet."

"Afraid so."

"You need me, boss?" Pugh said.

"Naw, I'll handle it."

"Good," Pugh said. "I've invited Scarlett out for a late-night snack after her shift ends."

Tully gave the nurse a wink. "Watch out for this guy. He's got a bad rep."

She laughed. "Don't you all?"

"Well, sure, but Brian is one of the worst."

Tully pulled into the K-Bar lot and parked. The lot was crowded with police cars, an ambulance, and a fire-station emergency team. Several police officers were standing around a pickup truck. Tim was standing next to Willy, who was still drunk but an interested observer of the crime scene. Tim glanced in Tully's direction and then started to walk over. Tully could now see the side of the truck. He groaned. The driver's-side window was a spiderweb of glass, with portions completely missing. He could see bullet holes in the blue door on the red truck. He'd told Lennie, "You can't be dumb." But did he listen?

Tim walked up. "We checked for the guy's

ID. He hasn't got any on him."

"His name is Lennie Frick, Tim. He lived at Four-oh-five East Sharp."

Tim took out his notebook and wrote the name and address down.

Tully said, "He did a bit of time a while back. He wasn't a bad guy, just a dumb one. He might have seen whoever did the killings up on Scotchman." He nodded toward the truck. "This pretty much proves it."

Tim looked up from his notebook. "So you think you know who did it?"

"Yeah, I'm pretty sure. I don't have any names, though. Not to mention proof."

"Things are pretty bad when a kid goes out for a six-pack of beer and gets blown away."

"Acme?"

"How did you know?"

"I'm psychic."

"Looks like the shooter used a .22," Tim said. "Very small bullet holes. I counted six. No casings anywhere. So it was probably a revolver. Strange thing is, nobody we've talked to heard any shots."

"I'm not surprised," Tully said. "I suspect the killer used a silencer."

"A silencer! Sounds like Blight City is getting into the big time."

■ ■ ■ ■

Tully slept most of the day on Saturday. That night he called Pete Reynolds. "Pete, any chance you could take me for a spin in your airplane tomorrow?"

"Why, sure, Bo. For some reason I had the idea you hated flying."

"I do, Pete, but there's some stuff I need to check out from the air. Just a hunch I have."

13

Sunday morning, Tully had no trouble containing his enthusiasm for the flight. He stopped at McDonald's and had his usual Egg McMuffin and coffee, then drove out to the airport. Pete was already there, tinkering with something on his Super Cub.

"Doing some major repairs, I see."

"Naw, nothing major. A bolt here, a nut there, that sort of thing. Where we headed today, Bo?"

"I'm trying to solve a crime. People are getting killed for no reason I can figure out. I could understand if they were bankers or lawyers or people of that ilk, but they are just poor dumb kids scarcely twenty years old, if that. Anyway, I think Scotchman Creek may hold an answer."

Pete tossed a wrench back in his toolbox. "I haven't fished Scotchman in years but I can tell you the lower part of that crick is one unholy mess. The beavers run a series of dams crisscrossing each other all through there. It's impossible even to find your way to the crick anymore. Beavers helped turn it into one giant swamp. Some places the water comes up to your armpits, and that's if you ain't standing in quicksand. It was that way thirty years ago and probably a lot worse now. I imagine the beavers flooded hundreds of acres since then. Some mighty fine timber locked away in there but the beavers made getting it out more expensive than it's worth."

"I guess beavers aren't totally useless, then."

"Easy for you to say, Bo."

A few minutes later they were on the tarmac, sitting shoulder to shoulder in the plane's cockpit. As far as Tully could tell, the Super Cub didn't bother to taxi but jumped into the air from a standstill, hurling him back into his seat.

"What kind of motor you got on this thing anyway, Pete?"

"The most powerful money can buy. No sense flying an underpowered aircraft, I always say. I tell you what, Bo, we'll circle around Scotchman Peak to warm up, and then cruise back down the crick away from the mountain. You see that clearing in those trees down there? Well, I had a chopper back

114

then and had to put it down in that very spot a couple summers ago."

"Wow! That clearing doesn't look anywhere big enough to land a helicopter in."

"Shoot, until I landed, there wasn't any clearing there at all! Flipped over and mowed down trees like tall grass."

"I see."

The plane swept up and around Scotchman Peak. At some points, the vertical rock slabs of the peak looked close enough for Tully to reach out and touch.

Pete pointed to the base of a sheer granite wall. "You see that little lake down there, Bo? You ever fished it?"

"No. I didn't even know it existed."

"Hardly anybody does. It's haunted."

"Haunted? I've never even heard of a haunted lake."

"I hiked in there, oh, it must be twenty-five years ago now. Had my youngest son, Alan, with me. It was one heck of a hike and we planned to spend a couple of days in there, camping and relaxing. Alan was about fourteen. You see how the trees are thick as fur on a dog's back and how they come right up to the edge of the water? Oh, shoot, we've gone too far. I'll take us around again."

Tully shook his head. "It's okay, Pete, I

saw the trees!"

The plane had already leaned over on its side as it made a sharp turn around the peak and back over the lake. Tully could now look straight down out his side window and see how close the trees came to the lake.

Pete tapped him on the shoulder. "You see, Bo? I can always take us around again."

"I see, Pete!"

Pete seemed to scratch an itch somewhere on his back while leveling off the plane. "Well, when Alan and I got to the lake, trout was rising all over it but the trees come down so close to the water we couldn't back-cast. There was a big snowbank at one end of the lake, almost like a glacier. So Alan fights his way through the trees and climbs out on the snow and then he's got plenty of room to cast, and right away he starts hauling in fish. I got a little frantic because I can't stand for one of my sons to outfish me. But then I found this narrow log stretching out into the water and I was able to walk out three-fourths of its length. The water was shallow under the log, maybe six inches deep, crystal clear, the stones on the bottom sharp as a picture. I make three or four casts and don't get a hit. Then I notice this little wake, like maybe a tiny, invisible shark fin traveling through the water. It starts out in the middle of the lake, makes a wide half circle, and comes right up under my feet. I'm looking straight down into that little wake, Bo, and you gotta believe there wasn't nothing in the middle of it, nothing making it that I could see. It was like an invisible finger had drawn it through the water. Well, I stood there a couple of seconds, trying to think what might make the thing, and I look out into the lake and another little wake has formed. And this one swings around in the opposite direction of the first one and comes right up under my feet! And Bo, I ain't makin' this up! There was nothing in the middle of that one either!"

"So what did you do?"

"I yelled at Alan, 'We going home, son! Grab your gear!' He yells back, 'How come, Pa?' and I yells, ' 'Cause this lake is haunted!' "

"You're telling me Alan didn't even question you about the lake's being haunted?"

"Nope, he never said a word about it, just packed up and started down the trail. Maybe it was mostly because he didn't want to be that far back in the mountains with a lunatic, I don't know. You're the only other person I've ever told about that lake being haunted. Alan's never mentioned it either."

I wish you hadn't told me, Tully thought.

"Later I heard the Indians wouldn't go within ten miles of that lake."

"I'm with the Indians," Tully said. "You don't suppose the haunt reaches this far up, do you, Pete?"

"Good point, Bo."

Pete leveled the plane and headed down Scotchman Creek, swooping in low over the trees. Because of the wings on the Super Cub, Tully couldn't see much of the creek below. He pulled his camera out of his kit. "Can you tilt the plane so I can see below the wing, Pete?"

"Tell you what, Bo. I'll circle the peak again and then turn her up on her side. That way you can photograph the whole of Scotchman Creek. You snap pictures like crazy and then you can examine them in comfort when you get back to the office."

"Sounds like a deal."

Pete revved up the engine, circled the peak, and brought the plane back over the creek on its side. Tully snapped pictures for all he was worth.

"You want to do that again?" Pete asked, leveling out the plane.

"No!"

"Good! My old flight instructor used to tell me never to do that. Said planes can drop right out of the air when you do. It's never happened to me, though, except that one time."

"I don't want to hear about it!"

14

By the time Tully got to the office Monday morning, his pulse had almost returned to normal. He walked over to Lurch and handed him the memory card from the camera. "See what you can do with these photos, if there are any. I haven't been able to make myself look at them."

"I'll run them through Photoshop, boss, and get them sharpened up."

"Good. Call me when you've got them ready. If they don't turn out, we may have to do the shoot over. You like to fly, Lurch?"

The Unit gave an exaggerated shudder. "You know I hate it!"

"I don't care. If the photos don't turn out, you're going up!"

Lurch slid the memory card into his computer. "Take my word for it, boss, they'll turn out."

Lurch's fingers began to fly over the keyboard. "And now somebody whacks

Lennie Frick. No way Lennie ever did anything to anybody to get taken out like that."

"You're right, Lurch. I don't know what's going on." Tully walked over to Daisy's desk. She was hunched over her computer, frowning in concentration. "You believe in water spirits, Daisy?"

"Hunh?" she said, glancing up.

"Never mind." He walked into his office.

He picked up his phone and dialed the Social Security office. A woman answered. "Social Security, Jennifer speaking."

"Jennifer, this is Sheriff Bo Tully."

"Hi, Sheriff. What can I do for you?"

"I've been thinking of switching sides and taking up crime. Now, suppose I stole my old father's Social Security check. How would I go about cashing it?"

Jennifer went into a brief description of how the crime might be pulled off. She explained that as soon as the legal recipient of the check notified Social Security he or she hadn't received the check, an investigation would take place to determine if and how the check had been stolen. "It would be very hard to cash the check without proper ID, Bo."

"Suppose I killed Pap. Then he couldn't complain. I now use his ID to cash the

121

check at a bank drive-through. How about that?"

"In that case, you might get away with it for a while, as long as the victim couldn't complain and you had the proper ID, say Pap's driver's license, that you could send into the teller."

"Thanks, Jennifer. I'd appreciate you not mentioning this call to anybody, just in case I decide to kill Pap for reasons other than his piddling Social Security check."

"I won't tell a soul, Bo. So, when are you thinking of switching over to crime?"

"I'll see how this week goes, sweetheart."

He hung up, slid his chair back, and propped his feet on his desk. He sat there tugging on his mustache while he thought about Orville Poulson and Ray Crockett. Orville had supposedly gone off on his endless trip in January, leaving Crockett in charge of the ranch. If Crockett had killed him, he could have buried Orville anywhere on the ranch and there would be no way to find the body. The ground would be frozen in January, though — impossible to dig a grave. He supposed Crockett could have hidden the body under some hay in the barn and let it freeze. Then he could have waited for the ground to thaw in the spring. Tully thought he might follow Etta Gorsich's suggestion and look under the house. The ground there wouldn't have been frozen in January. It might be tough to get a search warrant for a body when you don't even know if there is one. Still, maybe he could get a search warrant from Judge Patterson. As Daisy liked to point out, Patterson was the best possible kind of judge: old and senile and one who would give Tully anything he asked for. And some people thought the justice system had gone to hell. What did they know?

Lurch opened his door. "I've got those photos up on the computer, boss. You want to come take a look?"

Tully got up and walked with Lurch back to his computer. The photo on the screen was surprisingly sharp, considering the circumstances in which it had been taken.

"What's that thing hanging down in front of the lens?" Lurch asked.

"Probably my tongue." Tully could make out a large patch of swamp below. He switched to another photo and then worked through the series. "Perfect! Just as I suspected."

"What did you suspect, Bo?"

Just then Daisy walked across the room and said in a low voice, "An Angela Phelps to see you, boss."

Tully glanced across the briefing room. A woman stood there, tapping her foot in a way that suggested impatience. He vaguely wondered why Daisy hadn't simply yelled across the room in her usual fashion. She apparently read his mind.

"FBI," she whispered.

"You're in for it now, boss," the Unit said.

"Nothing I can't handle, Lurch. The agent is a woman, after all."

Lurch smiled and shook his head as if in disbelief.

Daisy returned to her desk and showed the agent into Tully's office. He strolled slowly across the briefing room and stuck his head in the door.

"Be right with you, miss."

The look on the agent's face suggested she intended to truck no nonsense from this cracker sheriff. He walked back over to Daisy's desk.

"Maybe I should let you handle this, Daisy," he whispered. "The agent appears a bit piqued."

"That's a mild way of putting it. I would say she's totally —"

Tully walked into his office without hearing the rest of Daisy's assessment.

"Agent Phelps," he said. "Very nice of you to drop by. Please have a chair. You are by far the most attractive FBI agent I've encountered so far."

"I am impervious to flattery, Sheriff Tully. So it's useless to try it on me. Furthermore, your other wiles are equally useless. I have read through the rather thick file we have on you, and even a much larger one we have on your father. Both are devoid of any evidence of your having ever given the slightest assistance to the FBI."

He pulled up a chair and sat down next to her. Her black hair, neatly coiffed, had a bit of gray threaded through it. She wore a crisp white blouse under her black suit jacket, and there was no wedding ring on her finger. She was definitely a prospect.

"I find that hard to believe," he said.

"That we've never had an iota of co-operation from either of you?"

"No, that you have a thick file on me. So, what can I do for you, Agent Phelps?"

"It's our understanding that you have recently had three murders in a national forest and somehow neglected to inform us. As you probably know, the FBI likes to be notified whenever there's a crime on federal land, particularly if guns are involved."

"I was just getting to that. Yes, I kept telling myself, I must get word of the killings to the FBI. And here you are already, Agent

Phelps, just as I was about to lift the phone and call."

"I bet. All right, tell me what happened, in case all the news accounts I've read are incorrect."

"I think the news accounts are surprisingly correct. Let me think. I have so many crimes going on I can hardly keep them straight. Okay, here goes. I had been working nights and days and weekends, so I decided to take Thursday of last week off and go huckleberry picking up on Scotchman Peak. That's when I discovered the three dead bodies in the huckleberry patch. All three had been shot in the back of the head. Young fellows, probably not even twenty yet. They appeared to have been farmworkers, guys who spent a lot of time working in the dirt. We have a few leads we're following up, but that's about it."

Agent Phelps scribbled furiously in her notepad. Tully could see she knew shorthand. "So, do you have any idea what the motive might have been?" she asked.

"Not a clue. It couldn't have been robbery. These guys probably hadn't seen a dime in the last six months. One of my associates claims it had to be money. My own guess is they knew something and were shot to shut them up."

126

"Anything else?"

Tully hesitated. He didn't want the FBI in town shaking things up and scaring off his criminals. "Listen, Angela, I'll tell you something but it's just a speculation of mine. Will you keep it under your hat until I get it checked out?"

"As you can see, Sheriff, I'm not wearing a hat. But if I were wearing one, I would keep your secret under it for a while. But you have to let me in on the investigation."

"I can do that. Can you stay in Blight City for a week or so?"

"I probably can, unless something or someone gets blown up somewhere else."

"Good. What I want to tell you is that I think there were four intended victims up at the huckleberry patch, but one of them got away. He was creased by a bullet and had the wound treated in emergency at the local hospital. I'm going out this afternoon to look for him. If we can find the fourth guy, if there is one, our case is solved, except for catching the killers. He'll at least know who the bad guys are. And let me say there is absolutely nothing to that other aspect of my fame with which you need concern yourself. I'm always a perfect gentleman." He watched her closely to see if the little grammatical flourish had made any impression. Apparently not. "If you would like to join me in my search, I would be most happy to have you along."

Agent Phelps smiled. She had perfect white teeth, a dimple in her left cheek, and deep blue eyes. She was surprisingly pretty when she smiled. "It's a deal, Sheriff."

15

A half hour later Tully and the FBI were cruising the neighborhood where Scotchman Peak Road crossed the railroad tracks into town. The street they drove on was unpaved and thick with dust. The houses were ancient and large, with numerous old vehicles parked out front. Several dried-up and weedy lawns were adorned with cars up on blocks. One yard contained an assortment of upscale motorcycles. Three men lounged on the porch steps, smoking and drinking beer.

"This looks like a good place to get some local information," Tully said, pulling over to the edge of the road.

"It looks more like a good place to get a serious beating," the agent said.

Tully got out. "It might be better if you stay in the car, Agent Phelps." She didn't object. Tully strolled up the walk. He heard her window go down, so she must have reached over and turned on the ignition key. He suspected she had also drawn her gun.

The three men eyed him coldly.

"Howdy, boys," he said. "Nice day. I see you're out getting yourselves a little sun."

"And a little privacy," one of them said. He had a ponytail that flopped over his shoulder as he started to get up.

The apparent boss of the group, a large, tattooed, bearded, and beaded man, put his hand on Ponytail's arm. Ponytail sat back down.

"Relax, Lefty," the big man said. "No point getting yourself knocked senseless before we even know what the sheriff wants. So, how you doin' these days, Bo?"

"Fair to middling, Mitch. You been staying out of trouble?"

"What do you think?"

"I think not, but I've got other things on my mind today."

"Wouldn't be those killings up on Scotchman, would it?"

Tully put his foot up on the porch's first step and rested his hands on the back of his leg. "Yeah, it would. And also the killing of Lennie the other night."

The big biker shook his head. "Lennie never hurt nobody in his entire life. He was dumb as a rock but he was okay. And he knew how to keep his mouth shut."

"You and your friends here probably even helped him with his beer-can collection."

"We did what we could."

"The killers up on Scotchman probably didn't know Lennie possessed the talent for keeping mum about what he observed. It's likely he saw them up on the road and could have identified them."

Mitch leaned forward. "How come they wiped out those kids? You got any idea, Bo?"

"I've got nothing, Mitch. Pap says it had to be money, but I bet the kids didn't have a penny among them. I figure they knew something and were killed to shut them up. These are bad guys who did it — no offense."

Mitch snuffed out his cigarette on the step and flicked the butt into the yard. "Well, I'd like to help you, Bo, but we haven't seen any strangers hanging about all summer. We hear anything about who killed Lennie, I'll get in touch."

"Good. I knew you would. But what I'm looking for right now is maybe a house where a bunch of kids might be hanging out, a bunch of young guys, maybe some girls, probably runaway kids with nowhere to go but who may be getting by in a big old house around here."

Mitch turned and looked at the skinny one of the three, a mop of orange hair ballooning out from his head. "Tell him, Red. You may need a favor from the sheriff someday."

Red's jaw sagged open. He slowly shook his head.

"I said tell him."

"Uh, sure, Sheriff," Red said. "That big old house down there on the corner." He pointed. "The one with the broken picket fence around it. Must be a dozen hippie kids staying there at times."

"Thanks. I'll remember this, Red. What's your last name?"

"Smith."

"I'd already guessed that." He reached down and shook Mitch's hand. "I appreciate the help."

"I only do it for Lennie."

"I know, Mitch. Surely you didn't expect me to think you were getting soft in your old age."

As Tully got back in the car he noticed the FBI agent slipping her gun back into her shoulder bag.

"I see you were ready for action, Agent Phelps."

"You may call me Angie, Sheriff. And yes, I was. That's a mean-looking bunch."

"Those boys not only look mean, they are.

I much prefer to deal with good guys, but good guys don't know anything."

"You're right about that. So, did you find out anything?" She kept her eyes on the bikers as Tully pulled out into the street.

"I found out what I was looking for, but I don't know if what I was looking for is what I need to be looking for."

"I can understand that."

Tully pointed to the house on the corner. "The bikers told me a bunch of hippie kids live there, probably mostly runaways or kids whose parents booted them out on the street. A boy with a bullet wound in his arm was picked up on the road down the mountain a ways from where the killings took place. The logging-truck driver who picked him up dropped him off in this neighborhood. So my hunch is he might at some point have lived at that house. Maybe he went back there after the shooting. Maybe he's still there."

He parked in front of the house with the broken picket fence. Agent Phelps got out with him.

"You don't have to bother with this," he told her.

"Yes, I do," she said. "I'm not along to observe Blight County law-enforcement methods."

He glanced at her as if surprised. "I thought you were."

"No."

"All right! Then I'll use my usual Blight County law-enforcement methods. I get results a lot quicker with them."

"That's my understanding, Sheriff."

"Call me Bo."

"Bo."

Tully knocked on the door. A girl's voice called from inside, "Who's there?"

"Sheriff Bo Tully."

"And FBI agent Angela Phelps!" Angie called out.

"There's nobody home!"

"I'll talk to you, then," Tully said, pushing open the screen door and stepping inside.

A teenage girl in tan shorts and a man's work shirt sat on a couch that looked as if it had spent several winters outdoors. "You can't just walk in here like you owned the place. Don't you need a warrant or something?"

"That's only on TV," Tully told her. "Besides, I'm not here to arrest anybody." He turned back to the door. "It's okay, Agent Phelps. This young lady invited us in."

Angie stepped in, shaking her head.

"I did not!" the girl said. She seemed to

relax a little upon seeing a woman. "I really don't know anything about anything. And I'll be in big trouble if anybody finds out I talked to the police."

"How old are you?" Angie asked.

"Twenty-one."

Angie held out her FBI identification. The girl bent over and examined it. "I never talked to anybody from the FBI before."

"What's your name?" the agent asked.

"Jenny."

"Well, Jenny, you tell us what we need to know, we'll take care of you."

"Yeah, right, in juvie!" She rolled her eyes.

"No, not in juvie," Tully said. "We'll find you a place that's safe and where you're free to go as you please." He pulled up a ratty-looking armchair and sat down gingerly.

"Yeah, I bet. So what do you want to know?"

"A young man stopped by here a while back. He had injured his arm and went down to the emergency room to get the wound treated. Is he still living here?"

"No."

"Listen, Jenny, I'm not looking for him because he broke any laws. I think he may be in danger."

A nervous look came over Jenny's face. "Everybody seems to be looking for him."

135

"Who else?"

"Some bad guys. Really bad guys. They burst in and searched the whole house, but he had left already. They had guns."

Tully was silent for a moment. "Do you know where he went?"

"No."

The FBI agent spoke up. "Jenny, it's very important that we find him before the bad guys do. Can you tell us his name?"

The girl stared at the agent, searching her face for some kind of assurance. Then she said, "Craig."

"What's his last name?"

Jenny thought for a moment. "Wilson, I think."

"Do his parents live around here?"

"I don't think he has any parents. He sometimes talked about an uncle, a long-haul truck driver. Craig said he planned on becoming a truck driver like his uncle. He worked all summer hoping he would make enough for a down payment on a truck."

The agent jotted something in her notebook. "Do you know where the uncle lives?"

"Spokane."

"Do you know his name?"

"No."

"Where do your parents live?"

"Don't have any." She looked about un-easily.

"What's your last name?"

"Smith."

Tully handed her his card. "Jenny Smith, you have been a big help. If you need anything at all, you call me. We'll take care of you."

She looked at the card in her hand. "Okay."

"It might be a good idea not to mention to your friends that we were here. If the bad guys come back and you need help in a hurry, run to the house down the street where the biker gang hangs out. The leader is Mitch. Tell him you're a friend of mine and he'll take care of you."

"I know who he is," she said. "He's scary."

Tully smiled. "He's scary all right, Jenny. But I'm a whole lot scarier, and Mitch knows it. He'll keep you safe."

Back in the car, Angie said, "I thought that was nice, the way you told Jenny to run into the arms of a biker gang if she gets scared."

Tully sighed. "Mitch will protect her."

"You could have taken her to child services."

"Arrest her, you mean. For all you know,

Jenny could be eighteen. She could be an adult."

They continued their argument all the way back to the courthouse. Tully introduced Angie to Daisy, Lurch, Herb, and a couple of deputies hanging out in the briefing room. He and Angie went into his office and he closed the door. She settled into the chair across the desk from him and he flopped into his chair.

"How tall are you?" he asked.

"Five eight. Why?"

"What's your shoe size?"

She eyed him skeptically. "None of your business."

Tully waved a hand as if to dismiss that idea. "Listen, I want you with me on the next phase of this investigation. That's a compliment, by the way. I've never before taken a woman with me on an investigation, particularly an FBI woman. Since you're the first, I want you to be properly outfit-ted."

"You're going to buy me an outfit?"

"Sure. Well, actually, the county is. So what's your shoe size?"

"Eight. I assure you, however, that the FBI is perfectly capable of buying me an outfit."

"Yeah, I know, but the Fed penny crunch-ers would demand a bunch of info and explanations and all that."

"Well, I suppose the county could loan me the outfit for a day."

"Now you're talking. So here's the plan. There's a swamp out north of town a ways. I have a feeling that swamp has something to do with the killings up on Scotchman."

"A swamp? A swamp was involved in the killings?"

Tully tapped a pencil on his desk. "Maybe. Years ago beavers built a dam across Scotchman Creek. The water backed up and flooded out the road, and the county had to raise the level of the road. Then the beavers built another dam and another dam, until they had dams stretching miles back through the woods. Other creeks fed into the whole mess. The area is impassable."

Angie leaned forward. "Let me see if I understand this. You think this swamp had something to do with killings that took place miles away, and now you and I are going to make our way into this impassable bog in search of something. Exactly what is this something?"

"I wish I knew. I flew over the area yesterday and shot a bunch of photos. I saw a few spots I want to check out and some things that looked like buildings. I don't know why someone would build anything out in the middle of a swamp."

"So what's the plan, Bo?"

"I'll pick you up at your hotel about eight tomorrow morning. You probably should wear work pants, if you have them."

"I always travel with a pair of jeans."

"Good. Do you have a hat with a brim on it?"

"How on earth could I forget an essential like that!"

Tully made himself a note. "I'll bring you a one-size-fits-all cap. My head lice have pretty much cleared up and I don't think you have to be concerned about them. The reason I mention a hat with a brim is that the mosquitoes may be fierce in the swamp. They'll lap up mosquito dope like it's good bourbon. The only way to keep them off you is to wear mosquito netting so it hangs down over the brim of the hat, but a cap will work. Wear a sweatshirt. It'll be hot but better than getting eaten alive. Otherwise, wear a shirt on top of a shirt. And wear gloves."

Angie shook her head and smiled. "This outing sounds like a lot of fun."

"Yeah, it's fairly typical of my workdays, imposing law and order on Blight County. You take care of your clothes and I'll bring everything else we need. Oh, and bring your hip boots."

"Let me see, I'm not sure where I left my hip boots. Now that I think of it, I don't own hip boots."

Tully laughed. "I can scarcely imagine an FBI agent without hip boots. I'll take care of the hip boots for you. Oh yeah, and come armed."

"I always come armed, Sheriff, particularly when I'm going to spend a day with a perfect gentleman." She flashed her smile again. "See you in the morning."

Agent Angela Phelps got up and left.

Tully stood in his doorway and watched Daisy watch her go.

Daisy turned and looked at him. "Nice tight skirt," she said. "And that FBI sure knows how to use it."

"Really?" Tully said. "I never noticed."

Daisy laughed. "That would be the first time in your life, boss."

"No, I missed you one day when you walked across the briefing room."

He went over to his desk and dialed Blight City General Hospital.

"Scarlett O'Ryan, please. Sheriff Bo Tully calling."

Scarlett came on the line. "Hi, Bo. What's up?"

"You're a fly-fisher, right?"

"Right."

"That means you have hip boots."

"Yeah. And waders too."

"Waders! They might be even better. I need to borrow them for an FBI agent who's about five eight with an eight shoe size."

"Sure, you can borrow them. Sounds like a pretty small FBI agent."

"This agent is a woman."

"I should have known. Anyway, sure, you can borrow the waders for her. They should fit. What's the big adventure?"

"Don't tell anyone, but we're going to investigate a swamp in the lower part of Scotchman Creek. On the other hand, if you don't hear from me by tomorrow night, you can tell someone. I suggest Brian Pugh. You know Brian. He's already saved my life a couple of times and should be good for one more."

"You got it, Bo. Swing by my place about eight tonight. I should be home by then and you can pick up the waders." She gave him her address.

Tully stopped at her apartment on his way home that evening.

She handed him the waders and invited him in for dinner.

"By all means. I could use a home-cooked

142

meal. What are we having?"

"Hungry-Man turkey dinners."

"One of my favorites."

Tully got home a little after midnight.

16

Tully picked up Angie at her hotel the next morning. She was dressed as he recommended. He handed her the cap and she adjusted it to fit as they drove.

"This will be my first job off-pavement," she told him. "I called my boss to report in, and he was thrilled to learn I was spending the day with you in a swamp. He wanted to know what we're looking for. I told him I didn't know and that I was simply following you. He said, 'Oh, great!' So the FBI is well aware of your activities and you can see the level of its appreciation."

"That's nice. I try my best to cooperate with the bureau every chance I get. You can't imagine how pleased I am it has such a good opinion of me. By the way, how did you slip up?"

"What do you mean?"

Tully smiled as he turned off onto the Scotchman Peak Road. "FBI agents are usually sent to Montana or Idaho as punishment for having slipped up. So how did you slip up?"

"Perhaps getting born female."

"That would be my guess."

"Well, I'll have you know the FBI doesn't punish agents. Furthermore, I have had a very successful career. The bureau has long had a special interest in Blight County, and that's why they sent one of their top agents to investigate a crime here."

Tully glanced over and saw that she was blushing.

"I see. Sorry I asked."

"You should be." She turned and stared out her side window. "And I did something really stupid."

"Ah. Well, being the perfect gentleman I am, I won't attempt a guess."

"Thanks."

Tully backed his Explorer into a turnout next to the swamp. As soon as they got out he expected mosquitoes to swarm around them in black, hungry, vibrating clouds. Nothing. While Angie pulled on her gloves, Tully draped the mosquito netting over her cap. He tucked the bottom of the netting into her collar, leaving enough to billow out around her head. Then he handed her the waders.

"I thought you were bringing hip boots."

"I prefer hip boots on women because they're a lot cuter than chest waders. The problem with hip boots, they're always one inch too short for the water." He handed her a strap with a buckle on one end. "Fasten this around your, uh, top, and it will keep most of the water out if you fall down."

Angie shook her head. "This is already so much fun I can hardly believe it. Aren't you going to put on some hip boots or waders?"

"Naw, I prefer to get by with as little as possible." He draped the mosquito netting over his hat and tucked the bottom into the sweatshirt he wore over his blue denim work shirt. "On the other hand, I can't stand mosquitoes. Why we're not being assaulted by them already, I don't know." He handed her a walking stick. "If you start to get sucked down by quicksand, hold the stick out to me. That way I can pull you out without getting too close."

"This gets better all the time."

"Doesn't it, though?"

Tully tried to take her by the hand but she shook him off. They went down a steep incline, sliding down on a carpet of pine needles and grabbing at tree branches to slow their momentum. The woods below were thick with trees and dark with shadows. Squirrels complained shrilly at their approach, and for several minutes birdsong died away as they thrashed their way through the trees. They came to an opening in the woods where towering ferns grew over mossy mounds that had once been logs, discarded in the distant past for some unknown reason. The moisture on the ferns soaked Tully sufficiently that he began to wish he too had worn waders. Through a gap in the trees sunlight flashed on water. They were approaching the beaver dams and already he could smell the swamp.

The first dam wound off through trees long dead and whitened with age. The beavers had woven brush, logs, and driftwood into a dam that somehow held back an immense body of water. He and Angie approached the dam from the bottom, with water cascading and spouting through billions of small openings. The sound was almost musical. Standing beneath the front of the dam, Tully could barely see over the top of it. He wondered what kind of blueprint beavers had for creating such a structure — or did they simply start aimlessly weaving stuff together until they had a dam?

Did they even think about creating a dam? Maybe dams were simply accidents that resulted from their fooling around, much like the Army Corps of Engineers' accomplishments.

Tully led Angie over to where the dam abutted the hill they had just descended. As they slowly worked their way out onto the dam, Tully explained the art of walking on beaver dams. Mid-lecture, one of his legs shot down, as far as his knee. As he tried to disentangle his foot from the network of willows, branches, and small dead trees, he told her, "Remember the words I used when my foot shot down this hole. They are very important when walking a beaver dam."

Angie laughed. "There were quite a few words, but I'll try to remember them. By the way, what is it we're supposed to be looking for?"

"A couple of islands." He ran his hands down his pant leg and squeezed out as much water as he could. The water wasn't stained with blood, even though his leg felt as if it should be. He hated pain without blood. "I spotted the islands from the air. One of them contained something that looked like a building, a structure of some kind anyway. I asked myself why anyone would build something out here in the middle of a swamp. There were some large patches of bare ground, too. As you can tell, any ground we can see that sticks up above the water is covered with grass three feet high. And there are some massive crops of cattails everywhere you look. If we get stranded out here, we can survive on cattail roots. Ever eat any cattail roots, Angie?"

"No. Have you?"

"No! I read a book one time that said they were edible. Of course, there's a big difference between good and edible. Edible, I think, only means you won't die from it."

Angie stumbled and fell against him. "Sorry, this is my first time on a beaver dam." She steadied herself. "At least I now know the words to say if one of my legs breaks through."

Tully smiled. "Yes, remember those words. They are very important. But perhaps we shouldn't be creating such a high profile of ourselves." His eyes scanned the edge of the woods. "There could be someone who doesn't want us out here poking around."

"Now you tell me."

"Yes, well, you never know. Let's walk below the dam. It's pretty watery down there, but nothing you shouldn't be able to handle with your waders."

"Sounds good to me."

They worked their way down the face of the dam. Some openings spurted water through with considerable force. After working their way to the base of the dam, they moved out away from the gushing water. The shallower channels of water scarcely rose to Tully's knees. It had been an unusual stroke of brilliance that made him think of the chest waders for Angie. If he had remembered a life preserver, he could have floated her across several of the deeper pools. Occasionally, he detected signs of dissatisfaction on the face of the FBI agent. Then a string of words suddenly erupted from her as she stumbled again.

"No, no," he said. "Use those words only when you step through a hole in a beaver dam."

"Very funny! I'll tell you something, Bo! This is the last time I let some cracker sheriff talk me into slogging my way through a swamp!"

Tully smiled. "It requires a certain charm and talent."

"What, wading through a swamp?"

"No, persuading a pretty woman to do it."

He heard a sharp crack somewhere above them on the backwater of the dam, but close. He automatically ducked, then turned to check on Angie. She was crouched down, the water almost to the top of her waders. A revolver had magically appeared in her right hand. "Was that shot intended for us?"

"Probably," he said. "But I don't think we need worry. Beavers are notoriously poor shots."

"Are you trying to be funny?"

"Yeah. Sorry about that. That crack you heard wasn't a gunshot. It was a beaver slapping his tail on the water. That's a warning to other beavers that there's danger in the area. Namely us."

"A beaver?"

"It's a bit different from a gunshot but close enough to get your attention. I imagine by now all beavers in the area have lit out for their hiding places."

Angie slowly straightened up and tucked her pistol down somewhere inside her chest waders. "Whew! I thought somebody had us. It was so close."

"You're not the only one," Tully said. "I imagine the crack of a beaver tail raised the hair of more than one mountain man trudging through hostile beaver country. Not all beavers are hostile, but some are."

They at last came to where the beaver dam abutted against a higher piece of land. Tully thought it must be one of the islands he had spotted from the air. Water gushed through the dam and they had to fight their way up through it. Before pushing to the top of the dam, Tully stuck his head up and looked around. They had reached an island all right, and he could see no sign of life, wild or otherwise. He climbed to the top of the dam.

"I'm pretty sure we're alone out here," he said, "but it might be a good idea to watch for any kind of movement. I don't mean just bad guys. This is a great place for moose. A cow moose and her calf would be particularly bad news. Actually, any moose is bad news."

Angie looked around, her hands on her hips. "Now you tell me! And here I was only worried about bears."

"Oh, I forgot to tell you about bears. We have only black bears in Blight County but they get pretty cantankerous this time of year. Definitely, watch out for bears."

"No grizzlies?"

"Oh, occasionally someone claims to have seen a grizzly, usually in the high country over by Montana."

Suddenly she yelled his name, her voice tinged with panic. Great, he thought, now she sees a bear.

"I'm sinking, Bo! I can't get my feet loose!"

"Don't move!" he shouted. "It may be quicksand!" He had never heard of any quicksand in Blight County but if there was any, count on an FBI agent to find it. He plunged down off the dam. Circling around so as not to be caught by whatever had grabbed Angie, he came in behind her, wrapped his arms around her lower abdomen, grabbed his left wrist with his right hand, and wrenched back. She came loose, making a kind of *oooffff*ing sound as they both fell over backward in the water.

"Are you hurt?" he asked, holding her on top of him while she caught her breath.

"No, I'm okay. I thought for a second I was a goner. Scared me. You squeezed the dickens out of me with that lower Heimlich. I hope the lady you borrowed these waders from isn't too good a friend."

"Why?"

"Don't ask."

"Oh no! I'm sorry!"

"Only kidding. I'm okay. The waders are okay."

He stretched out, now lying nearly flat in the water, still holding Angie. The water was warm and cushy and smelled of decay. It occurred to him he liked holding her. He had never held an FBI agent before. The agent seemed to like it, too.

"Let's get out of here," he said. "This swamp may swallow us up before we find what we're looking for. I know a good guide we can get cheap. He knows this swamp like the back of his grubby hand."

17

Angie stripped off her chest waders when they reached the Explorer. She opened the door to the cargo area and tossed them inside. Tully thought she had probably finished with waders forever. She was almost as wet as he was, no doubt because she hadn't tightened the chest strap sufficiently. Their clothes dried quickly in the heat of the car. He drove fast with all the windows open, the wind blasting them from all sides. He didn't want to explain that the air-conditioning on the Explorer hadn't worked in years. Who needs air-conditioning when you have windows? He turned north on US 95.

Angie stuck her hand out the open window and let it glide up and down in the wind as if it were a bird. "Where are we going now?"

"To see a fellow who probably knows that swamp better than anybody else."

"A friend of yours?"

"Sort of. I've locked him up a few times for poaching. He enjoyed the room service so much I could hardly keep him out of jail. I finally told the judge I'd had enough of Poke and we'd forget the bit of poaching he does to survive. I didn't get any complaint from the game warden either."

She pulled her hand inside. "Poke?"

"Yeah, Poke Wimsey. I think his actual first name is William, but Poke is all I've known him by. He told me one time he got the nickname when he was a young boy, because he was always late. Poke is never late anymore, because he never does anything he can be late for."

"He sounds like your kind of guy."

Tully ran up the windows. "He lives in a little log cabin back in the woods. I think it's on about a hundred acres of forest. He got the land by trading the old family homestead to the Forest Service. Most people around here are scared to death of him, the sensible ones anyway."

"He must be a real mountain man."

"Yeah, sort of. But he's a mountain man like you've never seen before. I doubt there's an ant or a spider or a wild plant in all hundred acres he doesn't know personally."

He turned off the highway onto a gravel road. There were farms on both sides. Presently, the forest started again and there were no more farms. The road turned into rutted dirt. Tully could see in the rearview mirror the dust curling up high behind them. After a couple of miles, he shifted into four-wheel drive.

The Explorer swerved in and out of the ruts. Then they came to a tree lying across the road. It was obvious the tree had been cut down so it would block off any stray traffic. Since nearly everyone in Blight County owned a chain saw, it was unusual that the tree had been allowed to remain where it was. Tully drove in and out of the ditch and into the woods, whipping the vehicle this way and that, and finally back to the road on the other side of the tree. Tracks indicated he was not the first to do so.

Angie turned and looked back at the tree. "Explain to me again, Bo, why the authorities allow someone to block a county road like that."

"It's simple enough. Beside the fact he doesn't mind in the least going to jail, Poke doesn't have any money, so it doesn't do any good to fine him. Furthermore, just about everybody in the county is afraid of him. No sensible person sees any reason to make an enemy of Poke. If you think about it, you realize people like him are about the only ones who achieve a complete state of freedom in modern society."

Angie shook her head. "I take it you're not afraid of this Poke."

Tully laughed. "You must think I'm stupid, Angie! Anybody with any sense is afraid of Poke!"

"I see. And exactly why is it we're going to visit him?"

"To see if he will guide us out into the swamp. The trick is not to give him any reason to kill us, pile some stones on our bodies and sink them somewhere out in a pool of quicksand, and let the water critters take care of any remains."

She gave a little shudder. "I'm so glad you eased my mind."

Tully turned off what remained of the road. The Explorer bumped and twisted through the woods until it came to a small clearing. Dozens of tree stumps dotted the clearing, in the middle of which sat a small log cabin. A man sat in a chair on the front porch. A rifle rested across his knees.

Tully stopped the Explorer and stared out the windshield at the man. "Sit here for a bit. I don't want to overwhelm him with company. I've left the motor running. If he kills me, whip the vehicle around and get out of here as fast as you can."

She heaved a sigh. "Great!"

"Oh, he isn't that bad. He used to be my high school biology teacher. It was the only class I ever got an A in. He told us he would kill any students who got less than a B, because they were too stupid to live and would eventually destroy the country. I'll give you a signal to come up to the porch."

"Wonderful. I can hardly wait."

He got out and walked toward the cabin. He could feel Poke watch him come, although Tully couldn't see the man's eyes under the brim of his faded and shapeless old felt hat. Poke had told Tully once he always liked to see a man's eyes. The old man stood up and grinned at him.

"Well, I'll be! Bo Tully! What brings you out this way?"

"A business proposition, Poke."

"Business? I ain't done a lick of business in fifty years. Who's that you got hiding in your rig? Tell him to show himself. I don't like folks hanging round I can't see."

Tully motioned for Angie to join him. She got slowly out of the vehicle, displaying no enthusiasm for the meeting.

"Gol-dang, Bo! You brought a woman! A

mighty fine-looking one at that."

"You know me, Poke. That's the only kind of woman I hang out with. She's what you might call a gentlewoman. So watch your language."

Tully noticed Angie was carrying her shoulder bag, with the flap unsnapped and her right hand resting on top of the bag. She gave him and Poke a faint smile as she came up.

"Angie, I'd like you to meet an old friend of mine, Poke Wimsey. Poke and I have known each other all my life. He's taught me everything I know about the woods and a bunch of other stuff too."

Poke removed his hat and gave Angie a shy grin. "Pleased to meet you, m'am. Not often I get to meet a pretty lady like you."

Tully thought Poke had probably learned his manners from Gene Autry movies.

"Why, thank you, Mr. Wimsey," Angie said, obviously relieved.

Poke pointed to the chair. "Have a seat."

"Oh, I can't take your chair."

"I can't have a lady standing while Bo and I sit here jawing. He claims he's got me a business proposition."

Angie sat down in the chair, leaning slightly forward, her hands on her lap, looking unbelievably prim.

"I do indeed, Poke," Tully said. "I want you to guide us out into the swamp."

"Oh, I can't do that. The swamp is dangerous. Folks go out in it and are never seen again."

"Yeah, I've heard the stories, mostly from you and Pap." He turned to Angie. "Pap is my father. He isn't at all the gentleman Poke is."

"I know," she said. "I've read his file."

"File?" Poke said. "What file is that?"

"The newspaper file," Tully said. "So what I'm offering, Poke — the county will pay you a hundred dollars a day to guide us around in the swamp."

"A hundred dollars a day! That's a powerful lot of money, Bo."

"There's a reason it's a lot of money. It could be dangerous."

"That's what I just said. It's dangerous. I reckon you're looking for those men who have been messing around out there all summer. They're a nasty lot. Met up with two of them once when I was out fishing and thought they were gonna kill me for the fun of it. I got out of there fast. I think they left a week or so ago. So I'll take you up on that hundred dollars a day."

Tully smiled. "Actually, Poke, the hundred dollars is for day. We want to go out only

161

during the night. It's fifty dollars a night."

"Fifty dollars! I lost fifty dollars just like that!" He snapped his fingers.

"Excuse me, Mr. Wimsey," Angie broke in. "Sheriff Tully is a little confused. Nights are twice as dangerous as days. So I believe the rate per night is two hundred dollars."

"Two hundred!" cried Poke. "That's more like it. I knew Bo was joking. There isn't any way I'd go out at night in a dangerous swamp for fifty dollars!"

Tully frowned at Angie. "Yes, I must have been confused. You see, Poke, Angie doesn't have to deal with a bunch of corrupt and vile and stingy county commissioners, so she can be much more generous with the county's money."

Angie ignored Tully and turned her whole attention to Poke. "Tell me more about the swamp's being dangerous, Mr. Wimsey."

Poke pulled over a block of firewood and sat down on it. "It started a long time ago. Some fellows were running a whiskey still out on one of the islands in the swamp. My popper was one of them. He was a young fellow back then, and his job was to sit out on the end of a dock and watch for revenuers. The head moonshiner gave him a shotgun and told him to shoot anybody he saw headed for the island. They worked only at night. So this night there was a moon out and it was pretty bright, but a fog was hanging low over the water. So Popper is sitting there, his legs dangling off the end of the dock, and he's bored to death because he never sees anything at all, let alone revenuers. All of a sudden he sees two boys gliding along on top the water. He knew right away they were ghosts, riding along on top of the water like that. He had never seen a ghost before and dropped his rifle right off the dock! Later, some of the moonshiners told him two boys had disappeared into the swamp and were never seen again, except for their ghosts that floated around the swamp from time to time. The current from Scotchman Crick flows right by the island, and that's what the ghosts were gliding along on."

"Good heavens!" Angie said. "Have you ever seen the ghosts yourself, Mr. Wimsey?"

"No, m'am, I haven't. And I don't want to either. But for two hundred dollars, I can chance it."

Tully was still scowling at Angie. "I bet you can, Poke. So when do we start?"

"Tonight's good for me."

"Can't do it tonight. I've got to drive into Spokane tomorrow, but I'll be back early in the afternoon. We could do it day after

163

tomorrow. At night, I mean. That all right with you, Poke?"

"I'll have to clear my busy schedule, but sure."

"Great!" Angie said. "What should we wear, Mr. Wimsey, hip boots or chest waders?"

"Shucks no! You wade around in that swamp, you'll get sucked down by quicksand!"

Angie looked at Tully and returned his frown. "Quicksand. I never would have thought of that."

"No, m'am, we won't be doing any wading. I've got a log raft, a nice deck on it made of planks. We'll go in comfort. I pole around out there a bit, fishing for bass and perch and crappies and checking out the smaller wildlife. Fishing is good but I don't go out until the folks leave. Here's an odd thing. The mosquitoes have been gone all summer. Last spring I started chewing up and swallowing a clove of garlic every morning to keep the skeeters off me and it worked like a charm."

"I noticed that," Tully said.

"You wouldn't think that would clear all of the skeeters out of the swamp, too, would you, Bo?"

"Wouldn't surprise me one bit." Tully

164

leaned back against the cabin wall. "You mention that the folks were gone from the swamp. What kind of folks?"

"Mean ones, at least the two I ran into last spring. After that I made a point of not running into them again."

"How many altogether, you guess?"

"Maybe a dozen. They seemed to be scattered about on the two islands. Some of them went back and forth to land with a big boat powered with a jet outboard the size of a hog. There's a short road into the swamp up where Scotchman runs in. They must haul the boat in and out with a trailer up there, but it's got to be one heck of a backing job. That road's as narrow and winding as the minds of our local politicians. No offense, Bo."

"None taken, Poke. A boat, hunh?"

"Yeah. Some of them stayed out on the island all summer."

Angie stood up and held out her hand for Poke to shake. "Thank you, Poke. Is it all right if I call you Poke?"

"Yes, m'am. A pretty lady like you can call me anything she likes, but Poke is fine."

"Good, Poke. And you call me Angie."

His grasp swallowed up her hand. "Mighty proud to know you, Angie. I hope you'll be coming along on our little adventure."

"I wouldn't miss it for anything. It'll make me feel just like Huck Finn, the log raft and all."

Tully got up and shook Poke's hand. "We definitely need to take Angie with us. She might turn out to be useful. We could throw her overboard if something leaps out of the swamp and attacks us. Anything you want us to bring?"

The old man screwed up his grizzled face in a thoughtful expression. "Just the money. Oh, some big flashlights would be good. And you might want to bring a rifle, Bo, if you've got one with iron sights. You can shoot a lot better and faster at night with iron sights than you can with a scope."

Tully frowned. "You think we might run into some bear or moose?"

"Oh, them, too. Just bring the rifle. A bottle of whiskey would be good too."

"Whiskey helps you see at night?"

"Not that I know of."

Driving back to town, Tully turned and grinned at Angie. "Well, what do you think of Poke?"

"I like him."

"You seemed to have fallen for his act."

She frowned at him. "What act is that?"

"That Poke is ignorant as a post."

"I didn't think any such thing."

166

"Well, it's all an act. He's written and published three books of poems. Besides that, he has hunted down and inventoried practically all the species of flora and fauna in the state. Recorded most of it on film."

"Actually, Bo, I did think he was wonderful, but I had no idea from talking to him that he was capable of such things. Never before in my whole life have I met anyone like Poke."

"He was some terrific high school teacher, I can tell you that."

"Is that why you're still afraid of him?"

"No! Didn't I tell you he's written three books of poems?"

They came to the log on the road and Tully bumped the Explorer out around it. "I've got a couple things I need to check out. One, I want to find the boy who escaped getting murdered up in the huckleberry patch. We find him, we've solved the murders. The other thing is I've got a missing person who also may have been murdered. His name is Orville Poulson. My only suspect in the case is his ranch caretaker, Ray Porter, aka Crockett. Tomorrow I want to check out the area in Spokane where Orville has his post office box."

"Check out the area where he has a post office box? That should be a big help."

"Yeah, well, you just wait and see, FBI person, what a cracker sheriff can come up with. And since you like odd characters so much, Angie, tomorrow I'll take you around to meet another really odd one. We may even take him along on our swamp excursion."

"Who, for heaven's sakes?"

"My father."

"The famous Pap Tully! I'd love to meet him!"

"If you like Poke Wimsey so much, you'll be absolutely delighted with Pap. I can't stand him myself but I suspect he's your kind of guy."

Angie laughed. "I can assure you I was much too young when the FBI went looking for Pap Tully. As I recall, all the bureau wanted Pap for was running houses of prostitution, illegal gambling, general corruption, and possibly murder."

Tully said, "I doubt if he ran anything, but he took a cut of everything. It made him rich. It's on record that he killed a number of people in his duties as sheriff of Blight County. Then there may be a number of off-record killings. As he will tell you and tell you and tell you, he was decorated by the governor for valor in the killing of three armed bank robbers. They hit him a number

168

of times before he killed them with a pump shotgun. Maybe that's why the bureau didn't charge him with anything."

"No, it didn't," she said, rummaging around in her shoulder bag. "I'm not sure why. One thing was, he simply disappeared. I guess we figured at least he was gone and we had better things to do."

"He went to Mexico until the heat cooled off. Loved it down there. Learned to speak a fair amount of Spanish. When you meet him, you may think he's an old-time hick sheriff, but he's actually very smart. With one exception, he's one of the smartest people I know."

Angie had turned down her visor and was using the mirror on the back to repair her lipstick. "So, did you get your intelligence from him, Bo?"

"Oh, no, he's not that smart. I got my intelligence from my mother, Rose. She's the real brains of the family. The only stupid thing she ever did was marry my old man twice. You ever been married, Angie? I notice you don't wear a ring."

She replaced the lipstick in her shoulder bag. "You noticed that, did you? No, I've never been married. I hate to tell you this, Bo, but the pickings are very thin out there when it comes to men. No offense."

"None taken."

"I've come close to getting married a couple of times, but the good one was killed in the line of duty, and the other one, a handsome devil, turned out to be one of the sorriest individuals I've ever laid eyes on. So now I've given up on men. You're perfectly safe with me, Bo."

He glanced at her. "Safe with you, Angie? That's a disappointment. I love a little danger when it comes to women. Here I've been giving you the full blast of my charm all day, apparently to no effect."

She laughed. "I wouldn't say that. When I was lying on top of you out there in the swamp, some old feelings came surging back. It really was quite nice. Then again, it might have been all that oozy stuff in the water."

After dropping Angie off at her hotel, Tully stopped by the office. The crew seemed glad to see him. The CSI Unit grabbed him by the arm and dragged him over to his corner. "Bo, you've got to do something about Daisy. She's been bossing us around like crazy. She'd have me sweeping the floor if I let her. After she wore us plumb out, she went down and laid into the prisoners. I think they're all scared to death of her, and

170

we've got a couple of really dangerous guys locked up. What do you think's wrong with her?"

Tully scratched his chin. "Women are awfully hard to figure, Lurch."

"I know. That's why I asked you."

"Don't worry. I'll take care of it. The old Tully magic."

He strolled across the briefing room and into his office. Daisy followed him in.

"You look exhausted, Bo."

"I am. Worst day of my life." He slumped into his chair. "The FBI is driving me up the wall. No offense to womanhood in general, but this female agent is making me crazy. You know I'm not fond of the FBI in the first place, but a woman agent, if you can imagine such a thing! This is the worst day I've had in fifteen years of law enforcement."

Daisy brightened. "Really, Bo, she's that bad?"

"You wouldn't believe it. I can see now why her home office sent her out into the wilderness, as she calls us. She thinks I'm a cracker sheriff. Does nothing but grind me down. I tell you, Daisy, this agent What's-Her-Name has just about put me off women for the rest of my life. I can't stand another day with her."

Daisy's mood had improved so much he was afraid he might have overdone it. So he got down to business. "What's happening here?"

"Oh, we had a bit of excitement. Some residents over on the north side called in and said somebody was firing an automatic weapon in the neighborhood."

Tully tapped a pencil on his desk. "Anything new?"

"Yeah. A little bit later I got a call from your friend the lunatic, Mitch Morgan. He said a girl by the name of Jenny came flying into his house this morning. A great place for a young girl, the hangout of a motorcycle gang. He said a pretty rough-looking guy was after her, so one of Mitch's gang laid down a line of bullets from an AK-47 in front of him. I sent Brian over to pick up the girl. He came back with both the girl and the AK-47. He said the bikers raised quite a fuss about the gun, but he told them he knew they had all done time, so it was illegal for them to have any kind of firearm, let alone an AK-47."

"Good for Pugh. I take it neither Pugh nor the girl was harmed. What did he do with Jenny?"

"Dropped her off at Rose's." Daisy looked pleased with herself.

Tully was shocked. "Mom's! She'd be better off with the motorcycle gang."

"Bo, your mom is the sweetest person in the entire world."

"Daisy, you are such a poor judge of character, I don't know why I ever leave you in charge."

She smiled. "Because I'm the smartest person you've got on your staff."

"Sad, isn't it?"

"You're starting to make me mad, Sheriff."

He laughed. "Only kidding, Daisy. You do a great job. Anyway, you're going to be in charge all day tomorrow. I have to go into Spokane and check out this Orville Poulson thing, and there's a chance I might be able to run down the kid who escaped getting murdered up in the huckleberry patch."

"You taking the lady agent with you?"

"Why on earth would I do that? One of the reasons I'm leaving at five in the morning is to avoid her. Anything else happening?"

"Hold on a sec." She walked back to her desk and returned with her stenographer's pad. Reading from it, she said, "Your fortune-teller wants you to give her a call."

"Daisy, one last time, she is not my fortune-teller. She isn't anybody's fortune-teller. Etta Gorsich is an investment consultant. At least she was when she lived in New York. What else?"

Tully got up and walked around his desk. Taking a ring of keys from his pocket, he unlocked the metal gun safe and took out a rifle with iron sights.

"Uh-oh," Daisy said. "This doesn't look good."

He picked up a box of shells and dropped it in his pocket. "Just a precaution."

Daisy looked back at her pad. "Mrs. Poulson stopped by again. You have to do something about her, Bo. That woman is totally distraught over her husband. Ex-husband. Probably dead husband."

"Give her a call, Daisy, and tell her to come see me next week. We may have this mystery solved in a few days. It won't bring Orville back but we should know what happened to him. Get a warrant to search under Orville's house for a body. You can take all day, because I won't be in the office at all tomorrow. You'll have to babysit the FBI agent while I'm in Spokane. Take her out to lunch, go shopping, anything. Think of something."

"Noooo!"

"Daisy, I can't take her to Spokane. She'll turn me into a raving lunatic."

"I don't care. You take her."

"Oh, all right, I suppose I have to. Just remember it's your fault if I come back with my nerves in shreds. Now get out of here. I have to make a phone call." He walked her to the door.

Daisy went back to her desk, smiling. From across the room, Lurch watched her. He looked at Bo still standing in the doorway to his office. The sheriff mouthed the phrase "The old Tully magic." Lurch smiled, shook his head, and went back to work.

Tully pulled out his little dog-eared notebook and thumbed through it until he found Mitch's number. He dialed.

Someone answered. "Yeah."

"Red, this is Sheriff Bo Tully. Mitch around?"

"Yeah. Hold on a sec, Bo."

Mitch came on. "Yo, Bo."

"Mitch, I appreciate your taking care of that little matter for me."

"No problem. The kid was terrified. Pugh came by and I turned her over to him. Hope that was okay."

"It was. Pugh is the best deputy I've got. Jenny's in good hands. Did you notice anything about the guy who was after her?"

"Not much. He drove a big ol' white pickup truck with dual tires. From behind, that truck looks like a fat old lady kicked in the butt. I hate those trucks."

"Me too. You get a license-plate number?"

"No. All I can tell you it was California. I doubt there's but one pickup like that in all Blight County, maybe in all of Idaho."

"California! Excellent, Mitch! By the way, I understand somebody laid down some suppressing fire from an AK-47. You know anything about that?"

"Nope. Must have been some guy passing through." Mitch turned away from the phone. "You know about anybody firing an AK-47, Red? Red says no, Bo. He don't know nothing about it."

"Tell Red whoever that fellow was, he probably saved Jenny."

"I'll tell him, Bo."

"I understand you lost an AK-47. I'll see if I can get it returned to you."

"No need, Bo. We've got a couple more."

Tully laughed. "Glad to hear it. I'll send Pugh around to pick them up."

"Yeah, well, you ever need another favor, Bo, just call."

"I'll do that, Mitch."

18

Tully met Angie at the hotel café shortly after five the next morning.

"You're a mighty early riser, Sheriff."

Tully pulled out a chair and sat down. "Yeah. And this is after I milked the cow, fed the chickens, and slopped the hogs. Did I mention my well is drying up and I have to dig a new one?"

Angie shook her head. "In one fell swoop, Bo, you wiped out any tiny bit of interest I might have had in you. The well finished it off."

He grabbed a menu from behind the napkin dispenser and perused it. "What, you don't like us farmers?"

"I was raised on a farm just like yours. Once I even helped my father dig a new well. It was ghastly! I get back there once a year to watch my folks work themselves to death. They claim to enjoy the life. Say it gives them a sense of independence." She

177

nibbled a triangle of toast.

"That's the same with me. If I get fired from my job as sheriff, I know I won't starve to death. Maybe I'll start making cheese from my goats' milk."

"You never mentioned goats."

"Goats easily slip your mind. I do have a treat waiting for you in Spokane, though. We'll stop by the art galley that handles my paintings, Jean Runyan's."

"Don't you have any of your paintings at home?"

"Oh, yeah, I have four of my best watercolors up on a wall of my bedroom."

Angie laughed. "That sounds a lot like bait, Bo."

"You think so, Angie? I suppose it's your FBI training that makes you so suspicious. No, the reason I have the paintings in the bedroom is, when I wake up in the morning and look at them, I think to myself, Dang, Bo, you are good! If you ever get sick of sheriffing, you can become a full-time painter."

Angie smiled. "I think that would make an awfully nice life, being a full-time artist."

"You forget the fun I have dealing with criminals day in and day out."

"Well, sure, there's that."

■ ■ ■ ■

Tully drove up US 95 to Coeur d'Alene and took I-90 into Spokane. He took the off-ramp at Main Street and drove north to the Meadow Park Shopping Center. A private post office with an outside entrance was housed in the mall. The First Miners Bank sat at the northern edge of the shopping center. Tully stopped in a parking area across from the post office.

He turned to Angie. "You really should come in with me. Pick up a few tips on crime investigation."

Angie opened her door. "Yeah, right. But it's a federal crime to mess with post offices. If you do anything illegal, I'll have to arrest you."

"Oh, in that case, maybe you should stay in the car."

"I'm going!"

An elderly clerk watched them enter. She seemed pleasant enough. A skinny young man with a shaved head messed with something in the back. Apparently, the business also did packaging, and he seemed to be wrapping up a small carton. Mailboxes covered one wall. Tully found the one with the number Ray Crockett had given him.

Walking over to the lady, he smiled at her as he took out his wallet and showed her his badge and identification. "Good morning, m'am. I'm Sheriff Bo Tully from Blight County, Idaho. This young lady is Agent Angela Phelps with the FBI. I wonder if you can tell us anything about a particular mailbox and the person who uses it."

"Good heavens, there are so many of them. People come and go all hours of the day and night."

"Your customers have access to their boxes at night?"

"Oh, yes. And on holidays. We close off this part of the shop when we're not here, but customers can still get their mail."

"Can you tell me when this box was first rented?" He handed her a slip of paper with the number 281 on it.

"Oh, yes. I'll check the records." She called to the young man. "Viral, come and talk to these officers while I go check some records."

Sullen and bored, Viral slouched up to the counter. "Yeah?"

Tully smiled. "I take it your folks own this postal station."

"Yep. How'd you guess that?"

Tully shook his hand. "Just lucky. Can you tell us anything about Box Two-eighty-one?"

"Ha! Well, nooo. It just sits there like all the other ones."

Tully gave him a grim smile. "Viral? Did I hear your name right?"

"Yup."

"Well, Viral, have you ever thought of going into law enforcement?"

The kid's expression brightened. "I've thought about it. Why?"

"Because as a sheriff I'm always on the lookout for sharp young fellows to hire as deputies. It's dangerous work but you look like the kind of fellow who could handle it."

"Yeah! I really could, Sheriff!"

Tully nodded. "I bet you could, Viral. If you ever get the urge, you come see me over in Blight City and we'll talk about it. Now about Box Two-eighty-one. Can you tell me anything about it?"

"Yeah, an old guy rented it a year or two ago. Ma can get you his name. He don't stop by to check it very often. See, it fills up with junk mail and we have to empty it out and put all the overflow in one of those big boxes over there on the side. We stick a key to the big box inside the little box. When he takes the mail out of the big box, the key stays stuck in it. Ma's got a way of taking the key out so we can use the big box again. Sometimes he has a younger guy pick up his mail. Probably his son. We don't see them very often. They must come mostly at night."

His mother came back and handed Tully a piece of paper. "I wrote his name down there, Sheriff."

Viral said, "The sheriff says he could use me in law enforcement, Ma."

"That's nice, dear. As you can see, Officers, the old fellow who rented the box, his name is Poulson, Orville Poulson. For a couple of months, he would stop in and pick up his mail. I think he travels a lot. I don't recall seeing him in a long while now, but somebody empties out both the boxes about once a month. He probably comes in at night."

Tully folded the paper and slipped it into the inside pocket of his jacket. "Thank you very much, m'am. You've been a big help. By the way, would you mind looking to see if there's anything in either box?"

She walked around behind a partition and apparently checked the box. "Other than a couple of local ads, both boxes are empty."

"Thank you, m'am." Interesting, he thought. There should have been at least one envelope for Crockett containing a Social Security check.

He and Angie walked out to the Explorer

and got in.

Angie said, "You were kidding, weren't you, about hiring Viral as a deputy?"

"Not at all. There's always a place in law enforcement for dumb. Right now I'm pretty low on dumb. They tend to get killed, rushing into situations the smarter deputies avoid."

"I see. You're really a softhearted kind of guy, aren't you, Bo?"

Tully started the car. "Indeed I am, Angie. I'm pleased you noticed." He nodded at the other side of the parking lot. "Now I want to talk to somebody at the bank over there. I see they have a couple of drive-ins." He drove across the parking lot.

Angie stayed in the car while he went in the bank. Tully assumed she was bored with practical police work. A perky young woman at a round desk asked if she could help him.

"I hope so," he said. He showed her his badge.

Her mouth gaped. "Maybe I should get the manager, sir."

"That won't be necessary. My question is very simple. I see you have a young fellow working the drive-in window. Now if someone drove up in that farthest station, the teller wouldn't be able to see the customer all that well. Now, suppose that customer sent a check in through that brass vacuum tube over there. Would the teller cash it?"

"Oh, not without proper ID."

Tully put his badge and ID back in his jacket's inside pocket. "Suppose the customer slid his driver's license into the carrier with the check."

"The teller would see if he had sufficient balance in the checking account to cover the check. If so, and the ID looked authentic, the teller would cash the check."

"Suppose it was a Social Security check."

"I think you had better talk to the manager about that."

"Oh, there's no need to bother him."

"It's a her."

"Sorry. You've been a great help, miss. Oh, I suppose the customer wouldn't have any problem depositing the Social Security check, if he had the proper deposit slip."

"I shouldn't think so. The teller would check the account, though, and ask the customer if he or she wanted a balance on the account. I know because I sometimes work the drive-in."

"I see. I bet you do a first-rate job, too."

She laughed. "Oh, you have to!"

"I hope you don't mind my saying, but you are an extremely attractive young lady."

She blushed. "Why, thank you. That's very nice."

"Oh, by the way, I don't suppose you could check your computer and see if a Mr. Orville Poulson has an account here."

"Oh, no. That would be strictly against our policy! I could be fired for that, I'm sure."

"In that case, I guess I will have to talk to the manager."

The girl punched a number on her phone. "Betty, there's a sheriff here at the front desk who would like to talk to you." She listened briefly and hung up the phone. "She'll be right out, Sheriff."

The manager came striding out of her office. She wore a nice gray suit, a businesslike white blouse, and rimless spectacles. She was quite attractive for a professional type, as Tully had expected. She held out her hand and Tully grabbed it and held it lightly in his grasp. She gave his hand a tug, but nothing Tully took for a serious effort. After a moment, he released her hand, but not until a slight blush appeared on the manager's cheeks. "Yes?" she said. "I'm Betty McFarland, the manager of the bank. May I be of help, sir?"

"I'm sure you may. This nice young lady here has provided me with all the informa-

185

tion she thought proper, and you should be very proud of her. She has refused to tell me if you have an account for a particular person, though. That is certainly sensible, but since I am law enforcement, I thought maybe you could provide me with that information."

She asked to see his ID. Tully showed it and his badge to her. "What is the name, Sheriff?"

"Orville Poulson."

She turned to the desk attendant. "Check for an account under that name, please, Janet." The manager looked over her shoulder at the computer screen. "Yes, we do have a checking account under that name."

"Excellent!" Tully said. "You've been a huge help."

They both beamed at him. Tully briefly thought maybe he should open an account there.

When he got out to the car, Angie was slipping her cell phone into her shoulder bag.

"How did that go?" she asked.

"Perfect. I'm beginning to see how Ray Porter, alias Crockett, has been pulling this off."

"Great," she said. "By the way, would you like to talk to Craig Wilson's uncle — one

Ted Wilson?"

Tully stared at her. "How on earth . . ."

"I won't bother you with the details, but I do have my connections. Right at this moment he's crossing the Indiana border into Illinois, hauling a generator the size of a small house on the back of his truck."

"You're amazing, Angie!"

She smiled. "You don't think the bureau would send a rank amateur to deal with the famous Bo Tully, do you?" She handed him a slip of paper with a number written on it. "I've been on the phone with Ted while you were fooling around in the bank, Sheriff. I saw you working your magic on those two ladies. The one is much too young for you, though."

Tully shook his head and dialed. A gruff voice answered. "Yeah?"

"Mr. Wilson?"

"Yep. You're the young lady's associate, I take it."

"Associate? Yes, that sounds about right."

"She sounds pretty nice on the phone. Don't ask me how the devil she hunted me down, but I'd hold on to that one if I was you."

"I'll definitely try to, Mr. Wilson. What I need to talk to you about is your nephew Craig."

Wilson swore. "What's he done now, he's got a sheriff after him? That boy will drive me crazy."

Tully could hear honking and the sound of cars whizzing by.

"I don't know anything he's done, Mr. Wilson. The reason I'm looking for him, I think he can help me solve a serious crime. For that same reason, I think the people who committed the crime may be looking for him, too. His life is in danger."

Wilson was silent for a long moment. "Sheriff, I haven't laid eyes on him all summer. I let him stay at my house in Spokane but he's been working over in Idaho on a farm or something. If he's his usual industrious self, he's probably not making much money. I told him in case of emergency I'd stuffed two hundred dollars up in the toe of one of my shoes in a closet off a bedroom he sometimes uses. It's for him and he knows where it is. The next-door neighbors have a key to my house. Get it from them and go check the shoe. If the money's gone, he came back and took it. Usually it's the police after him for some fool thing he's done. He's not smart enough to be a criminal and I hope he's finally realized that."

"You have any idea where he might be?"

"Like you said, he's on the run from

188

somebody. Go check the garage. There's a set of shelves on one side with camping gear on it. He loves backpacking. If the red backpack is gone, that's his."

"You got any idea where he might be?"

"What Idaho county you sheriff of?"

"Blight County."

"I'm sorry. Anyway, you familiar with Scotchman Peak?"

"You bet."

"Well, you drive up into the Hoodoo Mountains and there's a trailhead twenty miles north of Scotchman. It goes up to a little lake about straight down from the peak, the sheer side of the peak. You get an old Forest Service map, the trail should be marked on it. The trail is old. Used to go up to a lookout tower a few miles north of Scotchman. The tower's gone now, but you hit the top of that ridge, the going should be pretty easy until you drop down to the lake. There used to be a trail from the ridge down to the lake. There's half a dozen switchbacks leading down to the lake, with a lot of down timber across the trail. I don't think anybody ever goes into the lake anymore, but Craig and I fished it once. It would be a good place for Craig to hang out. I doubt anybody else would hike in there."

"I'm not surprised."

"That's my best guess, Sheriff. I think maybe Craig might have hit out for it and — wowee! Almost squished a hybrid. Bet I loosened up that fellow a bit. What was I saying? Oh, yeah, I've heard Craig talk about hiking in to the lake. If the money's run out of that job in Idaho and he's got the cops looking for him, I'd bet ten to one that's where he's gone. Nobody would think to find him in there."

"Thanks, Mr. Wilson. I'll check out the shoe and the garage. If I find Craig, I'll give you a call. Try not to squish any hybrids. Ford Explorers are okay, unless you come across one marked 'Sheriff.' "

Wilson gave Tully the address to his house and then beeped off.

Tully smiled at Angie. "Thanks to you and Mr. Wilson, we may have a lead. What do you think about a little backpacking, Angie?"

19

As they approached Blight City, Tully pulled into the long paved driveway that led up to Pap's castle. Tully believed Pap had built the huge house on a hill so that he could look out his front windows and survey what he regarded as his domain, a broad expanse that stretched out over much of Blight County, bordered on one side by Lake Blight, on another by the Snowy Mountains, and on another by the Hoodoo Mountains.

"Good heavens!" gasped Angie. "This is gorgeous!"

"Yes, it is. You might want to keep in mind, if you ever start looking for real men again, that when Pap dies I inherit all of this. Just thought I'd mention it."

She smiled. "I'll definitely keep it in mind, Bo."

"On the other hand, the way Pap is going, smoking and drinking and carousing all over the county, I suspect he'll never die, if for no other reason than just to torment me."

Angie laughed. "How old is he?"

"Just turned seventy-six. He stole a gorgeous young waitress from Dave's House of Fry about a year ago. Claims he hired her as his housekeeper. Turned out Deedee is now boss of the place and runs Pap around like he's a lowly servant. I love it."

"The House of Fry? I've heard it's the best restaurant in the county to eat."

They approached a wide parking area lit by several large lights on high poles. "It probably is. Claims to have the world's biggest and best chicken-fried steak. I've never found fault with the claim. The place is owned by a somewhat mysterious friend of mine, Dave Perkins. Dave pretends to be an Indian, but only because he wants to turn the House of Fry into a casino operated by his tribe of one."

Tully parked his battered old red Explorer next to Pap's most recent Mercedes, a small silver convertible that all by itself filled his son with unquenchable envy. And Tully didn't care that much about cars in the first place.

Angie dug a tube of lipstick out of her shoulder bag and, using the mirror on the back of the visor, refreshed her lips. The makeover completed, she examined it this way and that, shoved the visor back up, and said, "Your friend Dave sounds interesting. Why mysterious?"

"I'll give you one example. A while back we were eating in a little café up north, and a couple of young lumberjacks came in. They said we were eating at their table. Dave seems to be a mild-mannered guy, and he politely told them there were lots of other tables, choose one of them. The jacks told him they would move him to one of the other tables. One grabbed Dave around the neck and the other grabbed him around the waist and they started to lift. The next thing I knew, both men were lying on the floor behind Dave, both of them out cold and bleeding about the face. I was seated directly across from him and never saw him move. He was nibbling on a cracker. Now is that mysterious?"

"I would say it meets the definition. Do I get to meet him?"

"Before we get our recent murders taken care of, we'll no doubt bring him in as backup. I don't like to use him until a situation gets dangerous."

"You think this situation will get dangerous?"

"I'm sure of it." He jerked his thumb at the house. "Well, Angie, this is it. I might as well take you in and introduce you to Pap Tully. Don't expect too much."

"Oh, Bo, don't be silly. I'm sure meeting your father will be a treat."

Deedee answered Tully's knock on the door. "Oh, Bo! This is so great."

He introduced Angie. "She's an FBI agent."

"An FBI agent!" Deedee exclaimed. "My goodness, I've never met a real FBI agent before." She was shaking hands with Angie when Tully heard the rustle of paper, a piece of furniture knocked over, and the back door opening and slamming shut.

Tully rushed out the front door and around the side of the house. His father had already leaped into the convertible. Tully jerked open the passenger door. "Hold up, Pap. It's a woman agent. She's working with me. She's not after you. She just wants to meet you. You're her hero."

Pap turned off the convertible. "Really, Bo? You're not joshing me now, are you?"

"No. She's in town helping me on the killings up in the huckleberry patch."

"You say I'm her hero?" Pap looked skeptical but hopeful.

"She's read all about you. And she's very good-looking, particularly for an FBI agent. On the other hand, you should avoid committing any crimes while she's in town. I suspect she's the kind of agent who goes by the book."

Pap got out of the convertible. "If you say so, Bo, I'll check my list and eliminate any possible fed crimes. Good-looking, you say?"

"Yeah. Well, for a middle-aged lady. She's not one of those young hotties you're always checking out. Her name is Angela Phelps."

"Bo, any woman under sixty I consider a hottie. And quite a few over sixty."

They walked back into the house through the back door. Angie and Deedee were seated in the living room. Tully introduced Pap to Angie. She popped up from her seat and shook the old man's hand. "Mr. Tully, I have to tell you I've read everything ever written about you, and I have to say, you are a real-life legend."

Pap grinned. "A legend. Surely you exaggerate, Agent Phelps."

"Not a bit. And please call me Angie, sir. You son has been filling me in on even more of your extraordinary feats."

"Really? You sure it was Bo?"

"Yes indeed. Awarded a medal of valor by the governor. That's major, Mr. Tully. Major."

"They shot me three times," Pap said.

Tully shook his head. "Don't milk it, Pap. Which reminds me, Deedee, if you were thinking of serving tea, I take milk in mine."

"You are such a mind reader, Bo. Even though I hadn't mentioned it yet, I was very much thinking about offering you tea."

Pap said, "Would you like to see the medal of valor, Angie?"

Tully said, "Pap!"

"Indeed I would," Angie said. "And I don't know how a nice man like you, Pap, could raise such a grumpy son as Bo."

Tully rolled his eyes. Pap went off somewhere to retrieve his medal, and Deedee disappeared into the kitchen to make tea.

"You have quite the way with old men," Tully whispered to Angie.

She smiled. "It's my specialty. I'm surprised you didn't notice when we were in the swamp."

"Probably because I'm scarcely forty."

"Going on forty-three. Remember, I read your file, too."

Pap returned with the medal. Angie was impressed, perhaps overly impressed as far as Bo was concerned. Presently Deedee came in with a tray bearing a silver teapot and china cups. Tully could tell that Deedee had been upgrading Pap's lifestyle.

After both Deedee and Angie appeared to

be about finished making over Pap, Tully said to him, "Enough of this nonsense. I brought Angie over here only because I need some information from you about the swamp."

Pap chuckled. "I figured you was gettin' tired of these two beautiful women fussing over me." He grinned at the ladies. "Bo is about the most envious man you'll ever meet, when it comes to women."

"Yeah, yeah," Tully said. "Stop preening for a moment and tell me about the swamp."

"It's haunted." Pap settled back into his chair. "You know that, don't you, Bo?"

"So I've heard from Poke. In the past week I've heard about a haunted lake and now a haunted swamp."

"Poke's all right as far as he goes, but he don't go far. He's still too young."

"He was the first one to tell me it's haunted."

"Yep, and me and Eddie Muldoon was the fellas that haunted it. It's true, two young boys disappeared in the swamp, but that was long before Eddie and me came along. We was about ten, maybe even a little younger, when we heard that train robbers had buried their gold somewhere in the swamp shortly before they was killed by a posse. Now, you can check the old papers about the robbers, so you'll know that much is true."

Tully tugged on the droopy corner of his mustache. "I want to know all of it is true, Pap."

"It is, Bo, it is." Pap put his feet up on an ottoman, folded his hands on his belly, and prepared himself for storytelling. "Now shut up and let me get on with this. Where was I?"

"You and Crazy Eddie were ten," Deedee said.

"Right, we was about ten. I can't remember our exact ages. Anyway, Eddie found out about the robbers' treasure and came up with the idea we should build a raft and go look for it. We was in a powerful hurry to find the treasure because neither of us had a cent of money. The real Depression was going on at the time and any adults who had money, they didn't waste it on kids. Our raft wasn't much for show, because we built it out of cedar fence posts we borrowed from one of the Muldoon fences."

"Fully intending to replace them, no doubt," Tully said.

"You bet. Now are you going to let me tell this, or not?"

Angie and Deedee held fingers up to their lips, signaling Tully to be quiet. He expected

Deedee at least to be familiar with Pap's fantastical yarns by now. But he held his hands up in surrender.

"So," Pap continued, "we slid the raft into Scotchman Crick and both of us got on, one at each end. That's when we discovered we were one or two fence posts short, because the raft floated along about an inch underwater. In no time at all, we had drifted into the swamp. We had made ourselves some paddles, but they wasn't much good for steering a raft. You might think a crick would know its way through a swamp, but Scotchman don't. It would go this way for a while, and then we'd find that was a dead end, and then we'd turn and go a different way. Pretty soon evening came on, and after a while it got dark and the air took on a chill. The moon came out and the raft continued to drift this way and that, mist rising from the water, owls hooting, and every so often a goose or a duck would take off squawking like mad from right next to the raft and scare us half to death."

Tully smiled at Angie. She didn't notice. "All at once," Pap continued, "we look up ahead and see a big fire burning on an island and men outlined against the fire, rushing around, doing some kind of work. I whispered to Eddie, 'We're saved! Those fellas will get us out of here.' And he hisses back, 'No way! They'll kill us for sure. They got to be some kind of pirates! Just stand real still and maybe they won't notice us when we float by.' That's when I see the lookout. He's sittin' on the end of the dock with his legs dangling over the water and he's got a rifle across his lap."

"Wait a minute!" Tully exclaimed.

Deedee and Angie both shushed him.

Pap gave Tully a little grin and went back to his story. "Well, that lookout sees us and jumps up and his rifle falls into the water. He turns around and rushes back to the men working around the fire and he's telling what he saw and is pointing right at us. All the men stop what they're doing and stare out at us. But just then we drift into a patch of fog. One of the men takes off his hat and whips the lookout across the head with it. An hour or so later — it seemed like at least a year — we got back in the main current and floated out of the swamp. I ain't never told anybody about our little adventure before, because I figured nobody would believe it. But that's the way it happened."

Tully looked at Angie. Her mouth was gaping. FBI agents are such pushovers. He turned to Pap. "Angie and I have hired Poke to take us into the swamp on his raft tomorrow night. I've got this feeling there may be something in there that holds a clue to the murders up in the huckleberry patch."

Pap scratched his chin. "In that case, we'd definitely want Dave along."

"Poke did suggest I bring along a rifle with open sights. I've got my old Marlin .32 Special in the Explorer right now, but don't expect I'll have to use it. If the fellows I'm after are hanging around out there in the middle of the night, they're stupider than I think."

Pap looked over at Angie. "Well, I'd better go along. I don't trust you one minute out in a swamp with a pretty lady, Bo."

Angie laughed. "Thank you for the compliment, Pap, but I think I'll be safe with Bo. I'd love for you to come along, though."

Deedee said, "Oh, please take him! He needs a little excitement. And I need some peace and quiet."

Tully stretched and yawned. "I guess that settles it, Pap. You're going whether you want to or not."

Driving Angie back to her hotel, Tully said, "Well, what did you think of the famous Pap Tully?"

"I thought he was wonderful, Bo! I about fell over when he told that story about rafting through the swamp. It fit right into what Poke told us."

"You believed it, then, did you, Angie?"

"Why, yes, I did. Why wouldn't I?"

"I take it the FBI doesn't let you interrogate suspects."

"Now that you mention it, I haven't had that particular experience. Why do you ask?"

"No reason."

20

Tully was surprised the next morning to get a full cup of coffee out of one of the five coffee pumps, the first four of which, as usual, only *fiss*ed at him. The last one squirted out a full stream of black coffee. There was even a little pitcher of cream next to it.

"What's going on?" he said, looking around the briefing room at his troops. "You left me some coffee for a change."

Several of the deputies chuckled. Ernie Thorpe said, "It was just an oversight, boss."

"Not really, boss," Brian Pugh said. "It was Flo's idea that we start being nice to you. From now on, you've got your own coffee pump, filled with French roast, I believe. Flo says anybody who sneaks a cup out of it will have to deal with her."

Tully stuck his head into the radio room. Flo smiled at him.

"Thanks, Flo. It's nice to have someone

looking out for me."

"No problem, boss. I figured with you having to hang out all day with an FBI agent, you needed a little special care."

"Indeed I do." Tully guessed that she and Daisy had been discussing Angie. He glanced around the room. Daisy was at her desk. Lurch was in his corner. Undersheriff Herb Eliot was standing in front of the other deputies. "What's up, Herb?"

"I just finished my briefing, Bo. We've got some nut breaking into houses up on the north side. Because he doesn't seem to mind if folks are home, folks assume he's armed. So folks are going to shoot first and ask questions later."

"Yeah," Tully said, "and folks end up shooting one of their kids who gets up to go to the bathroom. Get over to the radio station, Herb, and be a guest on Jim Dinkum's morning show. Every idiot in town listens to it. Explain to our gun-happy populace that anyone firing a weapon inside the city limits for any reason will be in serious trouble."

"Got it, boss." Herb had settled into a chair and remained seated.

"One more thing," Tully said. "Everybody be on the lookout for a big white pickup truck with dual tires on the back and a

California plate. If you spot it, don't do anything, but try to get the plate number. Not a good idea to stop the truck. The occupants would shoot you dead in a second. I'm not sure what they're up to."

Ernie Thorpe raised his hand. "You got some evidence against these guys, Bo?"

"No, I don't. What's your point, Ernie?"

The briefing room erupted with laughter.

Tully went on. "We had one possible witness but somebody killed him. Pugh, if you're out in an unmarked car and happen to spot the pickup, you might follow it at a distance, try to find where they're holed up, but don't get close. You understand?"

"Got it, boss."

Ernie Thorpe said, "You think there's a connection between the break-in guy and the pickup folks, Bo?"

"Naw, I don't think so, Ernie. The break-in guy is some nut who doesn't realize some of our Blight County folks will shoot him dead and bury his body in the backyard before they eat breakfast."

Herb was still relaxing in a chair. Tully glared at him. "So why are you still sitting here, Herb? Get over to the radio station."

"Right, boss." Herb shoved himself up out of the chair and shuffled out.

Tully pointed to three deputies one after

the other. "Thorpe, Pugh, and Daisy, I want to see you three in my office. The rest of you guys hit the road and try not to get yourselves killed. Flesh wounds are okay, but nothing serious. Daisy will apply a Band-Aid. We can't afford more doctor bills."

The deputies shuffled off. Daisy, Brian, and Ernie went into the office, pulling in a couple of extra chairs. Tully sipped his coffee and set the cup on his desk. He flopped down in his office chair and studied the three deputies. He started with Daisy. "You get that warrant from Judge Patterson?"

"Yes. It's in my desk drawer. He was more picky than usual. He wanted to limit the search for the body to the house."

"Body?" Ernie Thorpe said. "What body?"

"Orville Poulson's," Tully said. "I have some information the body may be buried under the house. The ranch-sitter may have killed him, but I don't think so. He's a sociopath but not a killer."

Pugh leaned forward in his chair. "You think there's some connection between Orville Poulson and whoever blasted Lennie Frick?"

Thorpe added, "And the huckleberry murders?"

"Could be, but I don't have a clue. I think

206

the swamp has something to do with it, but I'm checking that out tonight."

"You taking the FBI lady?" Pugh asked.

Thanks a lot, Brian, Tully thought. He could feel Daisy's eyes boring into him. "The FBI lady is insisting on it. If we don't find anything tonight, maybe she'll head back to Boise tomorrow. Otherwise, I'm turning her over to you, Pugh. It's your turn to babysit her. I tried to get Daisy to do it but she refused."

"She's that bad, boss?" Ernie said.

"You wouldn't believe it, Ernie. Wait until you get a turn."

"Hey, I won't mind a bit! She's one good-looking woman!"

Pugh nudged Thorpe and rolled his eyes toward Daisy.

"I guess she's pretty pushy, though," Thorpe said. "I'm glad I don't have to babysit her."

"Anything else, boss?" Pugh said.

"Yeah," Tully said. "I just wanted to tell you, if I don't show up around here in the next day or so, go look in the swamp."

"Right, boss," Pugh said. "We'll drop everything and rush right out there." He and Thorpe got up and left.

Daisy said, "Mrs. Poulson is coming in this morning. Do you think we should tell

207

her about the search warrant?"

"I don't know. What do you think, Daisy?"

"She's pretty tough. It can't be any worse than what she's been going through, not knowing what's happened to Orville."

"Suppose we don't find anything under the house?"

Daisy thought for a moment, tapping her pencil on her stenographer's pad. "Then we bring in some cadaver dogs and search the property, square foot by square foot. I don't want Orville's wife to go through any more torment."

"Ex-wife," Tully corrected. "Besides, Daisy, we only have a warrant for the house."

Daisy smiled. "I lied, boss. I got the warrant for the whole property. And I notified the cadaver-dog guy we may need his services."

Tully erupted in exasperation. "Sometimes I wonder if I'm even needed around here! Daisy, that property is a thousand acres or more. It will cost the county a fortune to search the whole thing with cadaver dogs."

Daisy stood up and said calmly, "Well, if that's what we have to do, that's what we have to do." She turned and walked out.

Tully stared after her with a mixture of irritation and admiration. Who's running this outfit anyway? He shook his head. What would he do without Daisy? Might be nice to try, though. He picked up his phone and dialed Etta Gorsich's number.

21

Tully was lounging against the front of Crabbs when Etta drove into the parking lot. He thought it was too bad he didn't smoke cigarettes. That would give him a whole range of gestures. He could take the butt from his lips, snap it under a car with his fingers, exhale a stream of smoke, and squint at her through it. Now all he could do was stand up straight.

Walking up to him, Etta said, "You don't smoke, do you, Bo? That's one of the many things I like about you." She took his arm and led him toward the entrance. "Persons in your line of work usually inhale one cigarette after another. I don't blame them. The stress of the job must be awful."

"Nope, I don't smoke. Odd you should mention it. I guess the stress just comes and goes, Etta. Hey, it's good to see you. As always, you look fantastic." Tully had been working on attentive. She was wearing a white dress with a bright red scarf around her neck. She actually did look great. Etta was dynamite, even if she sometimes did give him the creeps. Like bringing up cigarettes just now.

The manager, Lester Cline, showed them to a table himself.

Etta said, "Why, this is the same table we sat at last time."

"Yes," Tully said. "It's now our special table. Right, Lester?"

"Indeed it is, sir." He gave a little bow. "Would you like your regulars?"

Etta laughed. "Actually, Lester, I would prefer something that doesn't require a bib."

"Indeed, madam! Perhaps our honey-basted chicken breast, potatoes au gratin, and a salad. What kind of dressing, madam?"

"Blue cheese, please."

"And you, sir?"

Tully scowled at him. "Lester, if you don't drop the phony maître d' act, I'll have to stand up and knock you down."

"Jeez, you're such a peasant, Bo. How can I elevate the sophistication of Crabbs with patrons like you?"

"Maybe by elevating the taste of the food. I'll have the same as Etta."

"Thank you. I should go off in a huff, Bo,

211

but I'm still working on my huff." Lester stomped toward the kitchen.

Tully said, "I liked him better when he was boosting cars."

Etta laughed and shook her head. "Blight seems such an unusual place. I guess that's why I like Idaho so much."

"You apparently haven't seen much of Idaho, Etta. Most of it is nothing like Blight."

"I suppose that's true. One of these days I'm going to get in my car and drive around the state for a whole month. Like to come along as a tour guide?"

"Sounds wonderful, Etta."

Lester returned with two glasses and a bottle of wine. "This is on the house, the best wine in Crabbs's cellar, I'm sorry to say." He nodded to Etta. "It's in honor of you, my dear, for having to put up with such a grouchy lunch guest."

Tully smiled. "Thank you, Lester. I'm sorry I was grouchy. Although I may try it again next time, if it gets us free wine."

Lester patted Tully on the shoulder. "Don't count on it, Sheriff."

"My goodness, Bo," Etta said. "A whole bottle of wine for just the two of us. You may have to drive me home."

Tully was pouring wine into one of the

glasses and some spurted over the side, making a small red stain on the tablecloth. He poured the other glass and then set the bottle down so that it covered the stain.

Etta said, "Well, what did you think about my idea of exploring Idaho for a month?"

Tully smiled at her. "I'm still stuck on your suggestion that I drive you home."

Etta smiled back. "First things first, of course. This is actually very good wine, don't you think, Bo?"

"I think it may be the best I've ever had."

He felt Etta's foot slide up his leg. She must have slipped her shoe off. And here he had a ton of work to do this afternoon. But, as Etta said, first things first.

Lester came rushing back to the table. "Bo, you must have your cell phone shut off. Daisy's calling you. She says it's urgent."

It better be, thought Tully. He pulled his phone out of his jacket pocket and dialed the office. "What's up?"

"We just had a fatal accident on the Cow Creek bridge. A car crashed through the side rail and went into the creek." Daisy sounded out of breath.

"That's quite a drop."

"Yes it is. Brian is out there and he says it's very suspicious. He wants you out there as soon as you can make it."

Tully stood up. "Tell him I'm on my way. Has Brian identified the victim?"

"Marge Poulson!"

He winced. "Oh, no!" He beeped off.

Staring blankly at Etta, he said, "I'm so sorry, but I have to run. We have a fatality out by the Cow Creek bridge."

"Good heavens!" Etta seemed almost in a trance, as if she were watching a tiny horror movie projected on a screen he couldn't see. Her face had turned pale.

"Etta?"

She blinked her eyes and stared up at him, as if for a moment wondering who he was. "Oh, Bo, go! Quickly! Don't worry about me."

What a crappy job, he thought, rushing out the door.

Ambulances, wreckers, fire-station and law-enforcement vehicles lined the road on both sides of the bridge, a section of which had been taken out. The pavement showed where a car had skidded toward what was now a break in the railing. Tully pulled up in front of an ambulance and got out. He walked around to the rear of the vehicle. The doors were open. He climbed in, having to stoop as he did so. The body was on a stretcher, covered by a wet white sheet.

Two feet protruded from under the sheet, one wearing a black high-heeled shoe, a style his mother would have referred to as "sensible." The other foot wore only a stocking. Water dripped from the feet to a puddle on the floor. The attendant stared at him. Tully said, "Pull the sheet down so I can see the face." The attendant did as he was told. It was Marge, all right. "Pull it back," he told the attendant. Climbing out of the ambulance, he almost bumped into the medical examiner. "Susan," he said. His voice was hoarse.

She was tucking her long blond hair up into a cap of some sort. "You knew her, Bo?"

"Yeah. She's Orville Poulson's ex-wife, Marge."

Susan said, "I talked to Brian and he said this was no accident. She was deliberately killed, according to the skid marks. Her car was forced off the bridge. Why would someone want to kill a little old lady? She couldn't do anybody any harm, and it doesn't look like she had much money or anything else."

Tully shook his head as if at a loss for any explanation. "Pap says people murder for two things, money and to shut someone up. In Marge's case, it had to be the latter. She has been hounding me for months to find her husband's murderer. So far we have no evidence he's been murdered or is even dead. We don't have a body."

Pugh had climbed up the embankment next to the bridge. He walked over to Susan and Tully. He was wet up to his waist.

Tully asked, "What do you think, Brian?"

The deputy wiped his brow. "Somebody killed her. The car was rammed from behind by a much larger vehicle. It hit her on the left rear corner and spun her around." He gestured toward the missing guardrail. "Then it pushed her car off the bridge backwards and it landed upside down in the creek. The car filled with water instantly but I think she probably was killed from the drop. I helped get her out of the vehicle and she felt like she was all broken up inside. Might even have been killed from the impact of the other vehicle hitting her."

Susan turned to Tully. "Any suspects, Bo? She's been talking to you about her missing husband, right?"

"Ex-husband. Yeah, I've got one suspect. He's someone she could cause a lot of trouble for. On the other hand, he doesn't seem the type to murder someone."

Susan frowned at him. "You think there's a type for murder?"

"I don't know. Given the right circumstances, I suppose just about anybody could kill somebody else. People are full of surprises. To kill a person like Marge, though, is pretty cold-blooded. My suspect is the only person I know who could profit from her death. He's not stupid, though. I'll bet you anything he's got an airtight alibi. If he does, you can be sure he had a hand in this. Knew it was going to happen. Maybe he even hired somebody to do it."

He turned to Pugh. "She was driving away from her home. You got any idea where she was headed?"

Pugh said, "I've got Ernie checking with her neighbors, to see if she had friends out this way or what. One of the neighbors said there was a big old farmhouse a few miles down that Marge rented out. She might have been headed there."

Tully tugged thoughtfully on the corner of his mustache. "I know who the renters are, Brian. Don't go near the place, except to drive by and see if a big white dual-tired pickup truck is parked there."

Pugh said, "You think . . . ?"

"It's possible, but don't do anything until I get back. I've got to go. I'm still pursuing the swamp thing. I'll meet you all back at the office in the morning."

22

Tully drove to his place. Bouncing down across the meadow toward his log house, he thought about how he and his wife, Ginger, had built it to become self-sufficient artists, he a painter and she a potter. After Ginger died, that dream evaporated, and he became one of a long line of Tullys to enter law enforcement. Eventually he became sheriff. He never locked the door on his house, even though his office often received reports of burglaries in the county. He opened the door and walked in. The huge painting he had made of Ginger hung on a wall by the door. It portrayed her coming through that very same door with a bouquet of wildflowers clutched in her hand, blond hair bobbing about her head as she smiled at him with the glee of a small child.

He went into his bedroom and changed into jeans, a work shirt, and hiking boots. He took a small bottle of OFF! from the medicine cabinet and rubbed the repellent into all exposed parts. He slipped his shoulder holster on, shoved in his Colt Commander, and snapped the retaining strap across it. Finally, he took his khaki vest out of the closet and put it on, mostly to cover the gun and shoulder holster. As always, the pistol gave him a certain sense of security. Then he drove over to the hotel and picked up Angie, who was waiting for him out on the sidewalk. She was dressed pretty much as himself, including a vest.

Climbing into the Explorer, Angie said, "I heard on the radio about Marge Poulson. That's really sad. The newscaster said officials believe it's a homicide. Any suspects?"

"Several," he said. "One is the sociopath Ray Porter, alias Crockett. As far as I know, he's the only one to profit from Marge's death. Maybe he did it. I've known a lot of murderers, though, and for some reason he doesn't fit. On the other hand, she was drawing a lot of attention to him. You never can tell. So are you ready for our great adventure?"

"As ready as I'll ever be. I've soaked myself head to foot in mosquito dope, just in case. And I've stuffed the mosquito netting in my bag."

He laughed. "Maybe Poke's right about

the mosquitoes, that they have simply dis-appeared."

"He should know. We certainly weren't bothered by them. But maybe they rest in the middle of the day."

"Mosquitoes never rest."

They picked up Pap. The old man climbed into the Explorer's backseat and laid his 30-30 rifle in the cargo section.

Tully said, "I see you brought some heavy artillery, Pap."

"Yep. I ain't shot that rifle in years but I nailed a paper plate to a tree out back of the house and put half a dozen rounds in the center of it. Made me think maybe I should go back to hunting with it. Killed my first deer with that rifle when I was eight years old."

Tully said, "Well, I hope you won't have need for it tonight. I've had enough killing for one day."

Pap tossed the seat belt to one side. "Yeah, I heard on the radio about the accident. Marge was a mighty nice woman, always helping somebody out."

"I don't think it was an accident, Pap."

"What! You think somebody deliberately killed her?"

"I'm sure of it."

"Well, if I ever found the —"

"Careful, Pap. We've got an FBI agent in the car. You don't want to give Angie the impression we have loose laws here in Blight County."

"Loose? We have a bunch of sissy laws around here anymore. You wouldn't believe the way it was in the old days, Angie."

"Oh, yes I do. Remember, Pap, I read the file on you."

He grinned. "You're so pretty, Angie, I keep forgetting you're an FBI agent."

Bo nudged her with his elbow. "Did his file say anything about his being a flagrant womanizer?"

"No way," Pap said. "The FBI doesn't invent a lot of nonsense like that, right, Angie?"

"That's right, Pap. We're only interested in the facts, nothing but the facts."

Poke was sitting on his front porch talking with Dave Perkins when they drove up.

Dave and Poke walked over and climbed into the backseat with Pap. Dave was dressed in his buckskin tracking clothes. They both laid rifles in the cargo area. Tully introduced Dave and Angie.

"We seem to be well armed for this expedition," Angie said. "Are we expecting trouble?"

"We always expect trouble when Bo invites us on an outing," Dave said.

Angie stuck out her hand toward the backseat. "You must be the famous tracker."

Dave took her hand and held it until she pulled away. He laughed. "Maybe the most famous tracker in Blight County. It's pretty easy to be famous here. I'm even famous for my chicken-fried steaks, which happen to be the best and largest in the world."

Tully said, "That's true. There's a big sign in front of his restaurant that says so."

"So, how much evidence could a person ask for?" Dave said.

"And the restaurant, if I recall," Angie said, "is Dave's House of Fry. Does that mean everything served there is fried?"

Dave shook his head. "Not at all. We also serve water, coffee, and salads. Sometimes we're accused of frying the coffee but that's an outright fabrication."

"I see. Contrary to what I've heard, you have a well-rounded menu."

"Yes, indeed. It's not my fault if some folks choose to die on the premises."

Poke said, "Good to see you, Pap," reaching over to shake his hand. "I didn't realize you were coming too."

"You know how it is, Poke, us old guys has got to keep an eye on the whippersnappers and not let them go off prowlin' 'round swamps on their own. You look fit as a fiddle. So where you taking us?"

"I'll show you. Bo, go back the way you came in and turn north on 95. You know where the Old Culvert Road is?"

"I do, Poke."

"Turn off on that. It'll take us in on the north side of the swamp. That's where the raft is tied up. No need to hurry. The sun's about to go down. We don't want to head out into the swamp till it's dark."

Tully turned in his seat and glanced back at Poke. "You think we might run into some of those folks you were telling me about?"

"I don't expect to, Bo. But some of them could still be hanging around. Looks as if we got enough firepower along to take care of ourselves no matter what shows up. You packing, Angie?"

She nodded. "You bet, Poke. I'm always packing."

"You're my kind of woman, Angie."

Pap grinned. "They don't make 'em like her no more, Poke. That's another thing I hate about modern times."

Tully twisted around so he could see into the backseat. "Would you two quit trying to hustle this FBI agent?"

223

"Keep out of this, Bo," Angie said. "I like it!"

Tully turned off on the Old Culvert Road. Half a mile in, they drove under a power line. "When did they put that in, Poke?"

"About five years ago."

"I see they used cedar poles. I thought anymore they used nothing but steel towers."

"Well, they used cedar poles on this one. I hate the steel towers. They're ugly as sin, in my opinion. Now right up ahead, Bo, there's kind of an opening in the woods. It used to be a road and it's kind of grown up, but your rig should be able to manage it."

The road wasn't any rougher than the drive into Poke's, and Tully guessed the brush scratched hardly any of the remaining red paint off the Explorer. Oh, well, time for the shop boys to repaint it anyway. The vehicle was at least eight years old. Any speed over sixty miles per hour, the front end shook like a rag in a dog's mouth. It was time the commissioners got him a new one anyway. How can you chase down a criminal if you can't drive over sixty? Tully had no intent of chasing down a criminal over sixty miles an hour or at any other speed. That's what deputies were for. They loved that sort of stuff.

As they drove farther, the trees got larger and the woods darker. The setting sun sucked the last of the daylight up the tree trunks as if they were giant straws. Night closed in around them. Suddenly there was water directly in front of them. Tully hit the brakes. His passengers nearly slid off their seats. Pap erupted in profanity and then apologized to Angie, but the outburst was probably nothing Angie hadn't heard many times before. In fact, Tully recalled a recent occasion when she used some of the words herself. Meanwhile the Explorer had stopped with its front wheels in the water, and Tully could feel them begin to sink into the mud. He hit the four-wheel-drive button and slammed into reverse. With a little spitting and howling, the vehicle climbed back onto dry ground.

Poke said, "I was going to tell you, Bo, I thought the swamp was just a lick or two ahead, but you got there before I could think of the words."

Tully shut off the engine and opened his door. "Thanks a lot, Poke. You managed to get us to the swamp sooner than I expected and closer than I wanted, but you got us here. How far does the swamp stretch out this way?"

The old man pointed directly ahead.

"Three or four miles across here at the bottom. Then it gets narrower as it stretches up toward Scotchman."

They got out and followed Poke along a game trail close to the water's edge. He stopped by a pile of brush.

"You fellows help me clean this off. I keep it hidden so youngsters don't come along and get hold of it."

"Good idea," Tully said. "They could take it out in the swamp and get lost or drowned."

"And leave my raft rotting away out there in the swamp!"

Once the brush was cleaned off, Tully gave a low whistle. "Poke, this is the finest raft I've ever seen."

Poke chuckled. "Isn't it, though? I put a lot of loving care into building it."

Tully said, "Those logs you've got under the deck, why, they're nearly as long and clean as those power-line poles we passed on our way in."

Poke smiled. "You think so, Bo? Why, that's mighty nice of you to say. Those power-company boys hauled a bunch of poles in one summer and left them lying on the ground for nearly a month. So when it came time to built my raft, I made some just like them. Oh, it was a powerful lot of work, Bo, but I got it done."

Tully nudged Angie. "Just look what a man can accomplish with nothing but a chain saw and an ax, if he puts his mind to it."

She didn't blink an eye. "It's the most beautiful raft I've ever seen, Poke."

"Thank you, Angie. Well, all aboard. The only downside of the raft, I haven't got a motor for it."

"A motor wouldn't do you any good anyway, Poke," Pap said. "Just make your raft go in circles. You know the only decent way to move a raft is to pole it."

"Danged if you're not right about that, Pap. I've got the poles leaning against a tree back in the woods. I'll go get 'em. They're long and slender and mighty fine to push with."

"Tamarack, I bet," Pap said. "The finest rafting poles there is."

"These have dried out for nearly three years. They're light as toothpicks and strong as iron. I'll go get them, if I can remember the tree I leaned them against."

Poke returned with two long, slender poles, one balanced over each shoulder. He gave them to Pap and Dave. "When you two get tired, Bo and I will take over."

Angie frowned at him. "Hey, where's my

pole, Poke?"

"You're a lady, Angie! I can't have a lady poling my raft. It would be bad luck for sure."

Angie sat down in a pout on the front of the raft and crossed her arms and legs. "This is the worst case of male chauvinism I've ever come across, Poke, and I've come across a lot of it. This raft doesn't move until I get my own pole."

Poke appeared about to panic. "No, you've got to be the lookout, Angie! You sit right there on the front of the raft and keep us from running into trees and stumps and stuff. I wouldn't trust anyone else here with that kind of responsibility. Now here's how the rest of us will do the poling. Pap, you pole on that side." He pointed. "Dave, pole the other. Now both of you drag your poles in the water to the front of the raft and push them down till you hit bottom. Then you lean into the pole and push the raft ahead with your feet as you walk to the back of the raft. You got that?" Dave and Pap nodded. "If Angie yells 'Pap,' that means Pap stops poling but Dave keeps on, and the raft will turn toward Pap's side. If she yells 'Dave,' he lets up and the raft turns his way."

Dave said, "Let me get this straight, Poke. We carry our poles back to the front of the raft each time we reach the back." He gave Tully a wink.

"No, no, no!" Poke yelled. "You drag the poles in the water. Otherwise you drip mud and swamp muck all over. We'd have a terrible mess in no time."

Pap said, "Been a long time since I rafted, Poke. Good thing you explained that to us."

Poke shook his head as if he couldn't believe the quality of crew he had brought aboard his raft. He walked over to Tully and tugged his sleeve. "You got a blanket in your rig? We need something to wrap the rifles in."

"You bet. I'll go get it." Tully walked back to the Explorer and returned with two blankets.

"You cold already, Poke?" Pap said. "I thought I could feel a bit of chill in the air myself."

"That's a mighty fine idea, Pap, and maybe I'll just take you up on it on our way back. For right now, though, I think we should roll the rifles up in the blankets so they don't slide all over the raft."

"I planned on being the lookout," Tully said. "Besides, Angie, if we get in a shootout, you won't be accustomed to my rifle."

"I qualified with one just like it at Quantico, Bo. It won't be a problem."

229

Pap and Dave began pushing the raft through the murky water while Poke wrapped the rifles in the blanket. Angie sat up front with her legs crossed in the lotus position. "I know the front of a boat is called a bow," she said. "What do you call the front of a raft?"

"Technically it's called the front of the raft," Tully said.

"We could use 'fore' and 'aft,' " Pap said.

"Somebody hand me that extra blanket to sit on," Angie said. "My aft is getting sore already."

Tully laughed. "Good! That will help keep our lookout awake." He picked up the blanket and tossed it to Angie.

The technique of driving the raft along was soon mastered. Once they were under way it glided along with surprising ease. A murky darkness seemed to be rising out of the swamp itself.

"Anyone bring Maglites?" Pap asked.

"Yeah," Tully said. "I've got a couple of them in my vest. But I'd just as soon not use them until I'm sure we're alone out here."

Angie said, "I've got one in my shoulder bag."

The full moon began to rise and bathe them in light. They could now see large patches of greenish scum on the water.

"What we looking for, exactly?" Pap asked as he poled toward the aft of the raft.

"I don't know exactly," Tully said. "There are two big islands out in the middle of the swamp. I flew over them a few days ago. There were structures of some kind on one and what appeared to be a lot of bare ground on both of them. I didn't see any sign of life. Somehow, I think this swamp has a connection to the killings up in the huckleberry patch on Scotchman. The only thing I can think is the swamp provided a cover for some kind of illegal activity. It's not the kind of place you have people just dropping in for tea or that sort of thing, so you wouldn't likely be bothered by visitors. If you have workers that don't want to be there, they probably aren't going to take off wading through the swamp. Who knows, there could be quicksand out there some-place."

"Yeah," Angie said, turning around to shoot Tully a look. "Wading off through the swamp would be really stupid, don't you think, Bo?"

"Maybe not if you wanted to get rid of somebody, Angie." He was crouched down next to the rifles.

"Yeah, like the FBI," she said. "One thing

we need to keep straight here, Bo, this is an FBI operation."

"It is?"

"If you think this swamp has something to do with the killings in a national forest, then those killings occurred in my domain. So I'm in charge of this little expedition. So far, I've been letting you wag me like the tail on a dog, but that's about to end."

"Well, let me say, a very attractive tail."

"No matter."

"Okay, Angie, you're in charge," he said. "What's our next step?"

Angie was apparently thinking of the next step when a Canada goose exploded out of the darkness right by her feet. It went honking off into the dark. Everything was quiet for a few moments. Then Pap said, "Angie, do they teach you those words at the FBI?"

"Some of them," she gasped out. "The rest I picked up from hanging out with low-lifes like you guys. I can tell you this, boys, if I ever see a goose walking across the road, I'm going to run him down!"

Pap laughed. "Is it a crime in Blight County, Bo, murdering a goose with a car?"

"As you are aware, Pap, hardly anything is a crime in Blight County."

As Pap and Dave began to get the hang of poling, the raft picked up momentum. Now they only had to give an occasional push with their poles to maintain the speed. Dave said, "It just occurred to me, Poke — what do we use for brakes on this raft?"

"Beats the heck out of me, Dave. I never had it moving this fast before. I guess whatever we run into will be our brake."

"In that case, I hope our lookout is keeping a sharp eye on everything up ahead."

Angie said, "So far we have missed a number of dead trees and stumps by several inches, but there's a big mass of something coming up."

"Better just let it drift in, guys," Tully said. "It must be one of the islands I want to check out."

"Good," Pap said. "I need a rest and a cigarette." He dug out the makings for one of his hand-rolleds and deftly put them together. He snapped the head of a kitchen match with a thumbnail and held the flame to the tip of his cigarette. Something cracked loudly in the direction of the island. Pap dropped his cigarette in the water and crouched down. The cigarette sizzled into silence.

Angie laughed. "Don't worry, Pap. It's only a beaver."

"Well, that beaver's a pretty good shot, because he dang near hit me. That bullet

233

whizzed by about half an inch from my ear."

Suddenly five shots were fired from the raft so fast they sounded as if they had come from an automatic weapon instead of a lever-action rifle. Tully spun around. He stared at Dave, who must have snatched his rifle from the blanket and fired. Tully had never heard a lever-action rifle fired so fast.

"I saw the muzzle flash near the top of the island," the tracker explained. "Probably didn't hit him but put enough lead in the air to scare him. We're not likely to hear from him again anytime soon."

Angie had her .38 out and pointed straight up. Any goose that surprises her now, Tully thought, is a dead goose.

23

The raft bumped gently into the shore. Angie stepped off, her pistol still out and pointed straight up. Pap and Bo each grabbed rifles. Dave reloaded his with shells he dug out of his pants pockets.

"What do you want me to do, Bo?" Poke asked.

"Stay with the raft. If it drifts off, we're stuck here."

Angie jumped to shore and then turned around. "Dave, would you hand me my shoulder bag?"

He picked it up. "Holy cow! What do you carry in here, Angie?"

"Among other things, my entire arsenal." She took the bag. "Thanks, Dave."

Pap and Angie crouched low as they moved slowly up the higher ground of the island. It had once been a hill, before the swamp backed up around it. Large evergreens cloaked its crown. Angie was in the lead. Tully moved up alongside her and whispered, "Unless the shooter has backup, he's probably on the other side of the island by now. Must have come out by boat."

Angie stopped and crouched. Tully crouched next to her. Pap came up behind them. "What's the plan?" he whispered.

"Beats me," Angie said. "What do you think, Bo?"

"I don't know. Where's Dave?"

"He's over to the right."

Tully said, "There must be something on this island somebody doesn't want us to see."

Pap whispered, "Well, we sure can't see much with only moonlight. You figure we're gonna stay here till morning, Bo?"

"I'm not sure that's a good idea. What do you think, Angie?"

"Beats me. I think we should at least push on to the top. That seems to be where the shot came from, according to Dave."

"Okay," Tully said, "but I'm taking the lead."

"Be my guest."

"Mine, too," Pap said.

They moved slowly up the slope. The ground near the top opened up beneath the towering ponderosas. It was free of brush and covered with a thick carpet of pine needles.

"Whoever shot at us must have taken off," Tully said from a crouch. Slowly he stood up.

"If the shooter came by boat, he's probably in it right now, headed back out of the swamp," Dave said. "Or maybe he's circling around to intercept us when we go back."

Pap peered off through the trees and clicked the safety on his rifle. "I don't think so." He pointed. A white object lay in the middle of a little clearing now bright in the moonlight. They moved toward it.

A large man wearing a white T-shirt lay on his back. Tully took out a Maglite and put the beam on him. The white shirt shimmered in the light. Blood oozed from two holes in his chest.

Tully bent to check his pulse, then straightened up. "You're some shot, Dave."

"Thanks. I've never cared much for killing, though."

Angie stared down at the body. "I've never killed anyone, but I've often wondered what it would be like."

"Like eating raw oysters," Pap said. "The first goes down pretty hard but the next ones are a lot easier. Pretty soon you start to like them."

Tully looked at him and shook his head.

"I can't stand raw oysters. Cooked ones either." He reached down and closed the dead man's eyes. "Remind me when I last deputized you, Dave."

"You bet. I think the last one should still be in effect."

"We'll refresh it if it isn't."

"Good."

Angie took out a handkerchief and used it to pick up the dead man's rifle. She held it under Tully's Maglite to examine it.

Tully nodded at the scope. "What kind is it, anyway?"

"A good one," Angie said. "I figured it had to be infrared, but it's just top-of-the-line regular."

She asked, "You think he's the only one on the island?"

"That would be my guess," Dave said. "He was obviously a lookout, sent here or left here to kill or scare off anybody who came poking around. I suspect he was low man on the totem pole. The top guys don't usually stand guard."

Pap and Tully grabbed the dead man's feet and started dragging him down the hill. Angie and Dave followed, carrying all the rifles.

When they got back to the raft, Poke said, "I didn't hear any shots. Who killed him?"

"Dave," Tully said. "From the raft."

Poke's whispered expletive was one of amazement. "I've never seen shooting like that in my entire life."

Pap said, "You never will again, Poke."

Angie looked back up toward the top of the island. "So you think our dead guy was the only person on the island."

"Probably," Tully said.

They built a driftwood fire in front of a log near the water and sat in a row with the blankets pulled over their shoulders. Tully said, "We should have remembered to bring hot dogs and buns."

"And marshmallows," Angie added. "Actually, I could go for a s'more right now."

"What's a s'more?" Pap asked.

"A Hershey bar and roasted marshmallow sandwiched between pieces of graham cracker," she said.

Tully shuddered. "Sounds illegal to me. That could kill an old man like Pap."

Pap tossed a piece of driftwood on the fire. "I was thinking the same thing, Bo. This here campfire reminds me of the time I took a prime elk steak out on a camping trip with Pinto Jack. It was pitch dark when I started cooking it over our campfire with only a flashlight to see by. I could hardly make out when the steak was done on the top side. When I turned it over it was burnt to a crisp

239

on the bottom — worse than that. It looked like a piece of cowhide tanned too long. But the top side was perfect — juicy and tender. So we cut it up in strips and ate it like watermelon slices, gnawing off the good side. It was the best steak I ever ate."

Poke said, "I've thrown away more than one piece of meat I thought was ruined, and I bet I could have sliced it up and eaten it like watermelon. You should write a cookbook, Pap."

"I keep thinking about it, Poke."

"Sounds illegal to me," Tully said, "Pap writing a cookbook."

Angie shook her head. "I hate all this talk about eating when we have a dead body lying behind us. On the other hand, is anyone interested in a turkey-and-bacon sandwich with cold curly fries?"

The three men stared at her. "You better not be just tormenting us, Angie," Dave said.

"Nope," she said. "I have five such sandwiches and fries, all prepared by the café at my hotel. They're for sale at a thousand dollars apiece. No checks, considering my present company."

"I want to believe it but I can't," Pap said.

Angie pulled a brown paper sack out of her shoulder bag and distributed the sandwiches. The men bit into them and groaned with pleasure.

Dave said, "No wonder that bag of yours was so heavy, Angie! I figured you planned to set up housekeeping out here."

"I'm afraid I forgot the glassware, Dave, but I did bring a bottle of bourbon." She took it from her bag and handed it to Pap. "So we'll all have to drink out of the bottle. I hope none of you have communicable diseases or are squeamish."

"Not me," Pap said. "But I may have to take up religion. This is a miracle!"

Later they relaxed around the campfire telling stories. Finally Tully said, "Dave's turn. Maybe he will enlighten us as to how he learned to shoot like that and all the martial-arts moves he obviously has."

Dave laughed. "I wouldn't call them martial arts, but I spent a year in Japan in the company of six Japanese gentlemen a good deal smaller than Angie. Every day for a year I paid them a lot of money to beat me senseless. They struck so fast you couldn't see them move. If you've ever seen a rattlesnake strike, that's how fast they were. By the end of the year, I was one massive ache but I could take out two of them in a match. I figured that was enough. From then on I worked on fleeing, just in case more than two bad guys showed up."

Pap laughed. "I myself have always favored fleeing right up front, so nobody gets confused about my intentions."

One by one they dozed off, curling up on the sand next to the campfire.

The following morning they explored the island. On the far side they found an aluminum canoe turned upside down on the bank, with one paddle under it, the transportation the sniper had apparently used to get through the swamp.

As Tully had noticed in his flight with Pete, a large portion of the island was barren of trees and the ground appeared to be tilled. There were watering cans scattered about near endless rows of stalks cut close to the ground. They found a pole shelter, the front of which was open. There were four cots inside containing a few rumpled blankets. In the back of the structure were half a dozen bags of commercial fertilizer and a pile of empty bags. The fire pit out front contained partially burned pizza boxes and wrappers for other fast foods.

"I guess we know what was going on here," Tully said. "They were growing marijuana. The murdered guys were the ones who took care of it, watering the plants and hoeing the weeds and so on. I figured them for farm laborers of some kind, and I guess that's what they were."

"Looks as if they weren't treated too badly," Angie said. "But there was no way off this island. They were essentially prisoners here."

"You don't feed prisoners pizza," Tully said.

"Yeah," Pap said. "And they could have got away if they wanted to. Something kept them here. My guess is they were promised a cut of the profits. So in the end the guys running the operation decided it would be cheaper to kill the help than pay them. It would also keep them from blabbing to the cops, if they got ripped off. It's like I always say, murder is done for money or to keep someone quiet. Hey, Angie, how about killing someone because you don't want to pay them?"

"It might seem the reasonable thing to do, if you don't mind murdering people."

Tully squatted down to get a closer look at some of the stubble. "If you're so smart, Pap, what happened to the marijuana?"

"Why, they harvested it! What do you think, Bo?"

"I think a couple tons of the stuff is pretty hard to market and distribute all at once."

"Yeah," Dave said, "but where are you going to store a couple tons of it? Haul it to a commercial warehouse? I don't think so."

Angie put her hands on her hips. "Okay, Bo, I'll say it. How about a barn?"

Tully stood up, wiping his hands on his jeans. "That's an A for Miss FBI. And who do we know has a barn? The Poulsons! And Mr. Poulson, the owner, happens to be missing and presumed dead, and his wife has been murdered. The ranch has a very large barn out behind his house. It is watched over by an extremely smooth sociopath by the name of Ray Porter, alias Ray Crockett, and Mr. Porter has a criminal record. Furthermore, who has been urging me to search the Poulson place for the body of Mr. Poulson? The ex–Mrs. Poulson! And what happened to her?"

"She was pushed off a bridge and killed," Pap said. "No doubt to take heat off the ranch. I hate to admit it, Bo, but you might be on your way to making a pretty decent sheriff."

Tully smiled. "Thanks, Pap. Maybe we'll get this whole business wrapped up in a couple of days."

Angie said, "And this ties into the huckleberry murders exactly how? Some evidence would be nice."

Tully tugged on the corner of his mustache. "Well, Angie, since the FBI probably isn't going to let us do this the Blight way, we'll have to tie the dead huckleberry pickers to the island. Maybe we can do that with fingerprints on the watering cans and whatnot. But to really pin the murders on the guys who ran the marijuana operation, we have to track down the fourth man, the kid who escaped the murder plot, Craig Wilson."

Angie said, "I don't think we'll solve anything standing around here."

"That's right," Poke said. "Besides, that fellow you killed, Dave, is going to spoil pretty fast in this heat."

"Not to mention I'm starving to death," Angie said. "Crabbs is actually starting to sound pretty good to me."

Tully laughed. "I hadn't realized we were undergoing such extreme hardship, Angie. Guys, we better get back to civilization before Angie goes even more wacko on us. Anyone who thinks Crabbs isn't so bad is right on the brink." He stepped backward and almost fell over something. "Hey, what's this?"

Pap bent over and looked at the little contraption. "It's a fogger!"

Dave scratched his head. "A fogger?

What's a fogger?"

Pap said, "It explains why there aren't any mosquitoes in the swamp! They put the fogger in their boat when the wind is just right and drive across one side of the swamp. It puts up a big cloud of insecticide that drifts across the swamp and kills all the mosquitoes and any innocent bug who happens to be passing through. Now that we've got the missing-mosquito mystery solved, shouldn't one of us paddle the canoe back?"

"Leave it for now," Tully said. "I want all of us to stick together."

They trooped back to the raft. They wrapped the body in one of the blankets and leaned the rifles against it. Angie and Poke took up their positions fore and aft, and Dave and Pap manned the poles. "Point the way, Poke," Tully said.

"What you mean, 'point the way,' Bo? Weren't you paying attention when you poled us in here?"

"No, I had you as a guide."

"Hunh. Well, it was dark. Let's see. I reckon if we head this way, it will take us back the way we came in."

"That way!" Pap shouted. "That ain't the way we come in."

"Well, what way you think it was, Pap, you're so dang smart?"

"I wasn't paying that much attention either. I figured you were the one knew the swamp."

"Shucks," Poke said. "I've never been in this far on a dark night with some fellow shooting at me."

Angie put her hands on her hips. "If all you mountain men will just shut up for a moment, I'll tell you how to get out of here. See that line of dead trees over there? Well, follow along them until we see green woods. Then we'll know we're moving along the north edge of the swamp. We keep the green trees off to our right until we see Bo's red Explorer."

"That's right," Tully said. "I was checking to see if Angie had been paying attention, and by golly, she was."

Angie rolled her eyes.

Two hours later they were in the Explorer and headed back to Poke's. Tully paid him three hundred dollars in cash and they were on their way into town.

"What we going to do with the stiff?" Pap asked.

"Drop him off at the medical examiner's."

"You think that's a good idea? In the old days we would have taken him out in the woods and buried him. Or we could have got some stones and sunk him in the

247

swamp."

Tully turned and looked back at him. "Have you forgotten we have an FBI agent in the car?"

"That's right," Angie said. "And I haven't quite acclimated myself to the Blight way."

"That's a pity," Pap said. "It complicates matters no end. Susan will want to know why we didn't leave the body where it was until she did her examination."

Tully said, "And I'll tell her we would have had to pole the raft back out of the swamp, drive into town, notify her and her crew, then lead them back to the swamp, load them all on the raft, pole them out to the island, and —"

"Stop!" Angie cried. "I get your point!"

"So the way we're going to work this," Tully said, "we're going to drop Angie off at her hotel, then we'll haul the body to the medical examiner, ask her to get some prints off it so maybe we can get an ID."

"Sounds good to me," Pap said.

"I don't think it sounds that great," Angie said. "I have to file a report."

"We'll give you everything you need for your report," Tully said. "You might have to write in a few gaps. You do know how to write gaps, don't you?"

"Actually, no."

"Well, I'll teach you. Here's your hotel."

Angie said, "I have to take a nap, to get my mind working again. Just remember, everything in my report has to be the truth."

"It'll be the truth."

"It better be. Otherwise I may find myself permanently assigned to Blight."

Tully and Pap stopped at the medical examiner's office. Tully went in and got Susan and two attendants with a stretcher on wheels.

"Jeez," one of the attendants said. "He's all bent."

Tully said, "Yeah, well, you'd be bent too if you had to ride in the cargo space of an Explorer for fifty miles. Strap him down and he'll flatten out nicely when he warms up. We just spent a night out in a swamp with him, so you can't expect everything."

"What happened?" Susan asked.

Tully told her his version and afterward said, "You understand that's our story, sweetheart, and we're sticking to it."

"The usual, in other words. So what do you want me to do?"

"I can give you the exact time of death, so you don't have to bother with that ugly stuff. You can do whatever you do, as long as you wait until I'm out of here. The main thing I want are the prints off the guy. Then get them over to Lurch so he can try to get an ID. I checked the guy's pockets but he didn't have a billfold. He paddled out to the island in a canoe, so there should be a vehicle somewhere near the swamp, unless he was dropped off by someone. In any case, this guy was involved in a large-scale marijuana operation. His pals are still out there running around and they're very dangerous."

"So you think you know who they are?"

Susan's attendants were strapping the corpse to an examination table behind them. The sounds were ugly. Tully shuddered. "Yeah. They're the same guys that killed the three kids up in the huckleberry patch. One down and two to go. The problem is, I just don't have proof of anything yet. There are some watering cans and various tools out on the island. I may get Lurch out there to see if he can pick up some prints. It hasn't rained since the murders, so the prints should be okay. That way we can tie the murdered guys to the island."

Susan laughed. "You're looking for proof, Bo? Whatever happened to the Blight way?"

"That's my fallback position."

He dropped Pap off at his house, then drove

over to the courthouse and went to the department office. The crew didn't even bother to look up. He tried his special coffee pump. It filled his cup with dark black coffee that smelled wonderful. He smiled in surprise. He stuck his head into the radio room. "This is great, Flo. I like having a pump all to myself."

She favored him with one of her blazing smiles. "Anybody else tries to use it, boss, I break his wrist."

Daisy looked up. "Well, it's about time, Sheriff. Do you ever think to turn on your phone, so we don't have to worry ourselves sick about you?"

"No way you need worry about me. Old Tully knows how to take care of himself. We did have to kill a fellow who took a shot at us. Pap was lighting one of his hand-rolleds in the dark, and I guess the assailant took offense and tried to gun the old man down. I can't say I blame him. Maybe he hated those hand-rolleds as much as I do. One of our party — not me — drilled the sniper through the chest. We've got some prints coming in from the dead guy, Lurch. You may be able to get an ID on him."

"Great," the Unit said. "I'll check with Susan."

Daisy said, "We should know better than

to let you out unsupervised."

Pugh asked, "You say you didn't shoot him, Bo?"

Tully shook his head. "No, Brian, Dave did. The guy was apparently aiming for my father and barely missed him. Anyway, we ended up spending the night in the swamp. Now, Brian, I want you to put together a raiding party for seven o'clock tonight. Get Ernie and six other deputies. Make sure they're well armed and wearing their vests. I'll be back at four and will fill you in then."

Daisy asked, "Can I go, Bo?"

"You bet, sweetheart. You're a deputy, after all. But wear your vest. There could be serious shooting."

She said, "You really think these guys are dumb enough to shoot, Bo?"

"I hope so. We'll have Dave along. Give him a call at the restaurant, just to remind him, Daisy. He's probably already sacked out, so give him a couple of hours. Oh, and be sure to inform the FBI. She'll be at her hotel. What's her name again?"

"Agent Angela Phelps."

"Right. Tell everybody we'll meet here at seven."

He walked into his office and shut the door. After staring at his painted window for a moment, he dug out his tattered pocket notebook. Putting his finger on a number in the book, he sat down and dialed the phone.

"Yeah?"

"Mitch?"

"No, I'll get him."

Mitch answered. "Yeah?"

"You guys need to hire a receptionist, Mitch. The phone manners there are terrible."

"I'd do that, if I was a rich sheriff. How you doin', Bo?"

"Fair to middling. I spent the night camping out and every bone and muscle I've got is aching. But enough about that. I've got a stiff down at the medical examiner's, and I was wondering if one of you sterling citizens might be able to identify him."

"We don't have any fresh kills, Bo, if that's what you're thinking."

"Remember the guy who chased the little girl into your house and one of your guys laid down a line in front of him from an AK-47? I'd like someone who saw the guy to come down and see if the stiff is the same fellow."

"One second, Bo."

Tully could tell Mitch had his hand over the mouthpiece but he could still hear him giving an order. Someone shouted, "What!

253

No way! I ain't!"

Mitch said, "Red will be right down, Bo. He may be a little worse for wear but he'll be right there."

"Thanks, Mitch. I appreciate it." He hung up.

Tully sighed and sipped his coffee. When he had drained the last drop of it, he wondered if Flo had got over her divorce from her loser husband. If so, she'd be a good prospect for a live-in housekeeper. On the other hand, he didn't think he could stand listening to a woman constantly gripe about her ex-husband. You need to let divorcées cool for about a year. He put both hands flat on his desk and slowly pushed himself up. He walked out into the briefing room and caught Pugh just as the deputy was leaving.

"Do we have Bev out of the hospital yet?"

"Yeah. She seems to be okay. I put her up at the Pine Creek Motel, on the county, of course."

"I hope you explained to her that it is not a good idea to start turning tricks out of there."

"That slipped my mind. But she talked about taking up a new trade."

"Good. In any case, I want you to pick her up and bring her down to the M.E.'s lab. I want to see if she can identify our dead body as one of the guys that used to sit at her table in Slade's."

"You got it, boss."

"See the two of you there in an hour."

As he walked by Daisy's desk she spun around on her little swivel chair and said, "Bo, you better go home and get some sleep. You look terrible."

"Maybe. First, though, I have to stop by the medical examiner's. One of the guys from Mitch's gang is coming down to see if he can identify the body. Brian's bringing our prostitute. It's a party. Then I'm headed home."

"Oh. Well, say hi to Susan for me."

"You bet," Tully said. "I suppose you know she hates me."

"Maybe. But single desperate women can get over hate for a man pretty fast."

He grinned at her. "I'll keep that in mind, Daisy."

Pleased to see her blush, he worried all the way out the door he might be hit in the back with a blunt object.

He was waiting in the reception room at the medical examiner's office when Red showed up outside on his motorcycle, the machine apparently unencumbered by a muffler. He walked out to meet the rider.

"Hey, Red, I expected you might bring along those AK-47s."

"What AK-47s you talking about, Sheriff? Pugh picked up the only one we had. Mitch said for me to tell you we didn't know what it was, so we used it for a wall hanging."

"I see. Well, I appreciate your stepping in and protecting Jenny."

"Anytime, Sheriff. She seemed like a real nice little girl. If one of the guys laid a finger on her, Mitch would have shot him dead on the spot. Well, I guess he would have taken him out behind the house and shot him there. He wouldn't want Jenny to see any more violence. Not that Mitch, being a convicted offender, has a gun. I don't want you to think that."

"I'm sure you don't, Red. Let's go in and have a look at the body."

Red raised his shoulders in a quivering shudder. "All right, but I really hate this, Sheriff. It gives me the creeps, having to look at a dead body. Still, it's better than being one, I suppose. Otherwise I wouldn't be here."

"Really. I'd guess you'd made a few of them in your day, Red."

"You got that wrong. I got no stomach for dead people."

They walked into the lab and Tully introduced Susan to Red. Then she whipped the sheet back off of the dead man's head. Red sucked in his breath and swayed back and forth. Tully grabbed his arm and steadied him.

Red gasped. "Cover it up!"

Susan pulled the sheet back over the body's head. Red turned and lunged back out into the reception room.

Tully thanked Susan and followed him out. The man was pale and shaky. "You okay, Red?"

"I hate this kind of stuff!"

"Maybe you should take up another line of work."

Red shuddered. "Don't think I ain't thought about it. I might even start at the junior college."

Tully sat down in a chair next to him. "Good idea, Red. What do you think you might major in?"

"Arithmetic."

"Arithmetic used to be a good major but now everybody's got a computer that does the adding and subtracting. You might want to look into something computers don't do, whatever that might be. So, did you recognize the corpse?"

"Yeah. He's the same guy chased the little girl."

Brian walked in with Bev. She gave Tully a big smile. The discoloration was almost gone from around her eye and she was much prettier than he remembered. She blurted out, "Oh, Sheriff! I'm so glad to see you. I can't begin to tell you how wonderful Brian's been to me. Why, he even —"

Pugh gave her a sharp look. "Enough about me, Bev! I think the sheriff has a little job for you."

"I do," Tully said. He took her by the hand, led her back into the lab, and introduced her to Susan. The M.E. pulled back the sheet.

Bev gasped and put her hand to her mouth. "That's the guy who hit me! His name is Stark. I think it's his last name. One of the other two called him that several times. He was a mean one, but I could tell he was scared of the other two."

Susan pulled the sheet back over the man's face. "Cause of death was two gunshot wounds to the chest. One bullet went clear through but we saved the other one. You want it, Bo?"

"Naw. Oh, on second thought, give it to me." She put the bullet in a tiny plastic envelope, sealed it shut, and handed it to him. He dropped it in his shirt pocket. He turned to Bev. "You getting along all right

258

financially?"

"Brian's been providing me with money but I need to get out and find a real job."

"No hurry, Bev. Take it easy for a few more days and get on your feet." He almost said, "instead of off them," but caught himself in time.

The room suddenly erupted in a thunderous roar. Both Tully and Pugh reached for their guns. Then Tully said, "Just Red, leaving on his motorcycle."

Pugh left with Bev. Tully turned his attention to Susan. "You happy these days?"

She smiled. "Do you really care, or are you just trying to be attentive?"

He laughed. "No, I really care, Susan. I want you to be happy. Anything new in your social life?"

"I've been out with another flyboy a couple of times. So far he hasn't set off any chimes. How about you?"

"Nope. Oh, there's one lady shows some interest in me. She's very nice but kind of sophisticated. A little weird, too."

"Etta Gorsich," Susan said.

"You must be psychic!"

"No, I just eat at Crabbs too. Lester has a thing for me and keeps me abreast of all your comings and goings."

"Lester!"

"You leave Lester alone, Bo! You give him any trouble, you'll have trouble with me. Like with the bullet you just slipped into your shirt pocket."

"Oh, don't worry about Lester. I'll leave him alone."

"So, what's it like, dating a fortune-teller?"

"As I get tired of repeating, Etta is not a fortune-teller. She's an investment consultant. She's a very nice lady and doesn't discuss cutting up dead people while we're having dinner. I've scarcely been able to eat a bite since my last dinner with you, and that was weeks ago."

"Well, you needed to lose a few pounds. And even if you don't believe it, I'm glad you found somebody."

"Thank you. And I'm glad you found yourself a new pilot. The free airfare will be nice. See if you can get tickets for Etta and me."

"What, there's not enough room for two on her broom?"

Tully thought it quite inappropriate for an attractive woman like Susan to laugh so hard while standing next to a dead person.

He went home and slept for two hours. Then he stopped by Angie's hotel to check on her. It was after two o'clock and she was seated in the café eating breakfast. He pulled up a chair across from her and sat down. "You recovered from our little adventure?"

"I just woke up! You, by the way, look terrible, Bo."

"Thanks." He picked a piece of bacon off her plate and munched it. A waiter came over.

"Would you like to order, sir?"

"Yeah, I would. I'll have what she's having."

"Good," Angie said. "Then I can consider that piece of bacon out on loan. So what's happening?"

Tully lowered his voice. "I'm putting together a raid. We're going to hit Orville Poulson's farm tonight."

"Tonight! What's the big hurry? Give us a chance to recover."

Tully eyed another piece of Angie's bacon but she snatched it up and started nibbling it. "Well, when Stark doesn't return — Stark, that's what we think the name of the dead guy is — then the other two are going to get concerned. They'll pull out as soon as they think the jig is up and they'll take their hemp with them."

"So what are you arresting them for?"

"Possession with intent to sell. A couple tons of the stuff, maybe more, that we

261

should find at the barn tonight. And after we've picked up a bit more evidence, murder. Daisy has cadaver dogs on order for tonight. I have a pretty solid hunch we'll find Orville's body under the house. As for the huckleberry murders, we might be able to hunt down Craig Wilson to identify the guys who killed his friends and shot him. I hope you're going to stay and help me with that."

She took a large bite of hash browns and spoke around it. "You're pretty sure the marijuana is stashed at Poulson's?"

"Yeah. Pretty sure, anyway. What better place than a barn?"

"So your sociopathic friend Crockett may be involved in this?"

"Yeah. In fact I suspect he's the brains. And he was sitting there on a ranch with a huge empty barn."

"So what's the plan?"

"As I told you, Daisy has arranged for cadaver dogs to accompany the troops. A judge has given her a warrant to search the whole ranch, but the main place I want them to check out is the crawl space under the house. Poulson disappeared in the winter, supposedly on a trip to Mexico, and the ground around the ranch would have been frozen solid. I don't think these are the kind of guys who would hack a grave out of frozen ground."

Tully's order arrived. Angie called in her bacon loan and nibbled it thoughtfully. Tully tasted the hash browns. Not perfect but not bad.

Angie said, "They could have stashed the body under some hay in the barn and waited for the ground to thaw in the spring. Then they could have dug an eight-foot-deep hole with a backhoe, and dumped the body in. I don't think cadaver dogs would detect him that deep down."

"Quit trying to confuse me, Angie."

"Why don't you just go up and use my room?"

Tully stared at her. "But I need sleep."

She laughed. "I promise I won't bother you. I'll go shopping. I have a very strong urge to go shopping."

Tully thought for a moment. "Okay, I'll take you up on your offer. Wake me at six?"

"You got it, Sheriff. What time's the raid?"

"We meet at my office at seven sharp."

"Good. Are you bringing Dave in on it?"

"Yeah. Dave would never forgive me if I didn't. He was pretty upset over the killings in the huckleberry patch."

Angie gave him her key and he went up to the room and used her phone to call Daisy.

"Boss! I thought you went home. I just tried to call you."

"No, I'm sleeping in town in the FBI's hotel room. It's not what you think, Daisy. It's perfectly innocent. She's gone! If you have any problems, call me here." He gave her the room number.

"Innocent? This would be a first, then?"

He groaned. "Daisy, get real. We've got some serious work going down tonight. Have the deputies ready to move at six forty-five, all of them armed to the teeth and wearing their vests. You, too. I know the vest conceals your nice little figure, but we all have to sacrifice. The cadaver dogs ready to go?"

"Straining at the leash, boss. So is their handler, Gordy something."

He yawned. "Good. I'm stopping in for a little visit with Ray Crockett about six-thirty. I'll be there when our guys come in to bust the joint. Oh, and the FBI wants in on this. If we nab the guys responsible for the huckleberry murders, they'll fall under Angie's province, if they're still alive. She can have them however they are. Have Ernie pick her up at her hotel."

"Got it, boss."

"Just remember, you're the best I've got, Daisy."

"How about the best you've ever had?"

"Let me mull that over." He hung up.

24

After telling the plan to his assembled deputies, Tully drove out to the ranch. As he turned into the gravel road he could see the large white boat parked in an open-sided shed out back. The barn loomed darkly behind it. He went up the walk and knocked on the door. Ray Crockett opened it. For a fraction of a second, his face registered shock. Then the old Ray took over. "My goodness, Sheriff, what brings you out at this hour?"

"Business, Ray, business."

"I hope you haven't come to haul me in for the murder of Orville Poulson."

"We'll have to talk about that, Ray." He glanced into the living room. A tall, slender, white-haired man was refreshing his drink at the small bar.

Ray Crockett said, "Sheriff Tully, I guess you and Orville Poulson already know each other."

The man turned around. "No need for an introduction, Ray," the man said, smiling. "Bo and I have known each other for twenty years or more."

Poulson strode across the living room and grabbed Tully by the hand. "Wonderful to see you, Bo! Can I fix you a drink?"

Tully couldn't find his voice for a moment, then croaked, "As a matter of fact, you can, Orville. Make it a large one. And while you're at it, I need to call my office. May I use your phone, Orville?"

"Help yourself, Sheriff. It's in the hallway."

Tully dialed the department number. Fortunately, Daisy was still there.

"Hi, boss. We're ready to move out."

"Cancel the cadaver dogs, Daisy."

"How come, Bo?"

"Don't ask questions. I'll tell you all about it tomorrow."

"Is the raid still on?"

"Yes. No point in canceling now."

He hung up.

Back in the living room, Orville was seated in a rocking chair, sipping his drink, and Crockett was on a sofa across from him.

"I can see you're as busy as always, Bo," Orville said. "Your drink's on the bar. Scotch straight up, as I recall."

Tully picked up the drink and took a gulp. "Perfect, Orville. Just what I needed. Yeah, I've got more than enough crime to keep me going. What brings you back?"

"A sad situation that you're familiar with. A friend got word to me about Marge's accident. True, we haven't been on the friendliest of terms since our divorce, but we were married almost forty years. Happily married for about thirty. Those years become a part of you. I was shaken to the core by the news. Now Ray tells me the paper says there's suspicion she was murdered. Is that right, Bo?"

"That's right. And we have evidence, too."

"Evidence! I can't for the life of me think of anything Marge might have done that someone would want to murder her."

Tully sipped his drink. "I can't either, Orville. But these days it takes very little to get someone murdered, even someone as sweet and innocent as Marge. I think there are people who viewed her as a nuisance and were concerned she might draw attention to their little scheme. Because she hadn't heard from you in a long while, she was sure you had been murdered and she was dead set on my arresting the person she thought had done it."

"For heaven's sakes, who did she think

that might be, Bo?"

Tully glanced at Ray, who was smiling at him.

Tully sighed. "Well, to be blunt about it, Orville, she thought it was Ray here. She thought he had killed you and buried you under the house. She was after me constantly to arrest Ray for your murder, but of course, your body was hard to find since you were wearing it."

Ray continued to smile and Orville shook his head. "She must have been teched, Bo. Maybe the divorce was harder on her than I thought. I know she didn't like the idea of me trusting the whole ranch to Ray here, but shoot, I even trust my Social Security checks to him. He must have a dozen of them stashed away for me."

Tully glanced at Ray. He had stopped smiling. "Sounds to me as if you've put a lot of trust in Ray."

"Why not, Bo? He's one of the nicest people I've ever come across."

A low rumbling came from behind the house. Ray got up, walked into the kitchen, and looked out a window. "Oh, it's just some fellows who came to pick up their boat. They said they didn't have any place to park it and wanted to know if they could leave it in your shed, Orville. I said, 'Sure.'

Hope that was okay."

"Okay with me," Orville said. "There's no walls on the shed so their boat's not very secure. Used to be a kid around here who stole anything not nailed down, so I hope they didn't leave any valuables in the boat."

Ray said, "Orville, the guy who owns the boat is headed for the back door. I'd better step out and talk to him. Uh, Sheriff, is something wrong?"

"If you're referring to the gun I have trained on your head, Ray, yes, indeed, something is wrong."

Orville gasped out, "Wha— ?"

Then came a rasping blast from a bullhorn: "Gentlemen, stand right where you are! Raise your hands, put them behind your heads, lace your fingers together, and drop to your knees! Nobody move!"

"What on earth!" Orville said.

"No problem," Tully said. "Just remain seated, Orville, and we'll get this all straightened out. Find yourself a chair, Ray. This may take a while."

Tully walked into the kitchen and looked out the back window. A large moving van had pulled in behind a white pickup. A deputy with a shotgun was standing over two men on their knees in the beams of the pickup's headlights. Tiny moths flitted about them. Pugh was handcuffing another man, apparently the driver of the van. The man shouted something at Pugh. Not a good idea. Pugh said something to him. The man sat down on the ground. Ernie Thorpe came running from the barn. Dave Perkins was just getting out of his car. Angie emerged from the passenger side. Dave walked over to Pugh. Thorpe was waving his hands and telling them something. Dave shook his head. Pugh turned and looked toward the house. He wasn't happy. He pointed to the back door. Thorpe came running over. Tully let him in.

"I hate to tell you this, boss, but there's not so much as a toke of marijuana anywhere in the barn!"

"What!"

They both turned.

Orville was standing there. "Marijuana in my barn? What on earth are you saying, young man?"

Thorpe looked at Tully. The sheriff shrugged helplessly and nodded for his deputy to reply.

Thorpe's voice was shaky. "Uh, we had a suspicion that marijuana was being stored in your barn, sir. But . . . but we couldn't find any."

"I should think not!" Orville said.

Thorpe shook his head and went out to talk to Pugh.

Tully heard the front door open and close. Then it opened again. He walked into the front room. Ray was backing in through the door followed by Daisy, who held the muzzle of her revolver practically on his forehead.

Daisy said, "I caught this fellow sneaking out, boss. I thought maybe you wanted him to stick around."

"Good idea, Daisy. Where were you going, Ray?"

"With all the excitement, I needed a breath of fresh air. I was only stepping out to the porch."

"Stay seated until we get this mess straightened out. Daisy, shoot him if he moves. Ray, what's that moving van doing out there?"

"Beats me, Sheriff. I don't need it. Everything I own will fit in my car. Maybe they got the wrong address."

Orville said, "Bo, I hope you can explain all of this."

"I hope so, too, Orville. What we know is that there was a large marijuana harvest near here and it had to be stored somewhere. For a number of reasons, we thought it had to be in your barn."

Orville stared at him. "In my barn? Bo, I've got *three* barns on the ranch. The one right here, another out in the meadow, and one down by the river."

Tully felt his jaw start to sag. "Three barns!" he said. "Just one moment, Orville. I have to speak to one of my deputies."

He stepped to the back door and yelled, "Thorpe!"

The deputy came running over. "There are three barns," Tully said.

"Two more barns!" Thorpe blurted out.

"Yes, one in a meadow and one down by the river. Check them out. Fast! I don't know how long I can go without my heart beating."

Thorpe signaled two deputies to follow him. The three of them climbed into a department Explorer and roared off toward the river.

Ray shouted at him from the living room. "I think you're supposed to have a search warrant, Sheriff!"

Orville, who had followed Tully, said, "Surely you have a search warrant, Bo."

"Of course I have a search warrant." He pulled a warrant from his inside jacket pocket and started to hand it to Orville. "Oh, wrong one. This one's for your body."

"For my body?"

"Never mind. Here's the one to search for marijuana."

Angie walked in the back door, showing her FBI identification. "Looks as if you have everything under control, Bo."

"I hope," he said weakly. He introduced her to Orville.

"The FBI!" cried the old man.

"Orville!" Angie cried. She shook her head and said to Tully, "Pugh got the names of the guys in the pickup, Stanley Kruger and Rupert Quince, both from Los Angeles."

Tully said, "Orville, it's a long story, and I can't tell you the whole thing now. But as soon as we have time, we'll be able to explain everything to you, right, Angie?"

"I hope so."

Pugh stepped in behind Angie. "I'm loading up our two murder suspects, Bo. What do you say I swing by the motel and see if Bev can identify Stanley Kruger and Rupert Quince as the guys at Slade's? That will tie them to Stark and the swamp."

Angie said, "Those two are mine, Deputy. Take them to jail. I'll interview them tomorrow."

Pugh looked at Tully for confirmation.

"Yeah, take them to jail, but let Bev look at them first. Don't let them see her, though. Right at the moment I'm not sure if we can hold them."

"Maybe they'll make a break for it," Pugh said.

"We're not that lucky, Brian. Lock them up in separate cells, far apart so they can't communicate."

"Jeez, boss, all the cells are already full."

"Well, stack some of the regulars and put each of these guys in a cell by himself."

Angie said, "And Sheriff, I don't want you talking to either of them unless I'm there."

"Perish the thought, Angie. Since the huckleberry murders were in your domain, why don't you ride in with Pugh, just to make sure they arrive at the jail safely?"

"Actually, I think it would be a better idea if Dave followed Pugh in. I'll ride shotgun with him."

I guess you have to be a tracker, Tully thought. "Fine. Just remember, I want them to arrive at the jail alive. Tell Dave that."

Tully and Orville walked back into the living room. Ray was sitting on the couch with his head in his hands. He looked up. "Sheriff, I didn't have anything to do with the killings up on Scotchman."

"Killings?" Orville said. "What killings?"

Tully said, "Three young guys were murdered up in a huckleberry patch. We think they were used all summer to cultivate a

275

marijuana crop out on islands in the swamp. When their bosses didn't need them anymore, they executed them."

"Executed them! Why on earth . . ."

"I'm not sure, Orville. Maybe only because they didn't need them anymore. Pap thinks it was because of either money or silence or maybe both. I do have a question for you, Orville."

"What's that?"

"How did you get around down in Mexico? You drive, or what?"

"Drive! In Mexico? No way! Even if my eyesight and nerves were that good, I don't think I could manage it. No, I fly down and take cabs and buses and trains. It's a lot safer for the Mexicans."

"So you didn't need your driver's license?"

"No, I've got my passport. That's all the identification I need."

"So your driver's license is here someplace."

"Right. I left it in a drawer in my bedroom. Why all the interest in my driver's license?"

Tully looked over at Ray, who seemed to be shrinking into the cushions of the sofa. "I'll tell you later, Orville."

Tully heard a vehicle roar into the backyard and stop. He glanced out a window. Ernie Thorpe got out of a department

Explorer and ran in through the back door.

"We got them, boss! The barn in the meadow is chockfull of weed. I left two deputies to guard it with their lives. Dave Perkins checked out the boat and found some marijuana seed there. I had two deputies search the boat before him, and they came up with nothing. Dave is something else. We've got them!"

Tully wondered for a moment if Dave's boat search involved something of the Blight way. Naw.

Dave came in. He was dressed in jeans, a gray suede jacket, and a black turtleneck. He looked terrific. Tully thought maybe that was his secret, high fashion. Dave said, "Bo, we're about to head in. Angie and I will follow Pugh, just to make sure the bad guys don't escape. Or try to escape. Pugh is still upset about the huckleberry murders."

"Yeah, it won't hurt to keep an extra eye on Pugh."

Tully turned to Ernie. "Good work, Thorpe! We're back in business. Round up the van driver and anybody else you find in the neighborhood and have some deputies haul them to jail."

He walked back into the living room. "Daisy, put your cuffs on Crockett and take him in. You need a backup?"

"What do you think, boss?"

Tully looked at Crockett. "Naw."

She cuffed Crockett behind his back and herded him out to her patrol car.

Tully went out in the backyard and found Thorpe. "Ernie, I'm leaving you in charge here. You and some of the deputies will have to spend the night. I'm headed home to bed. I'm wiped out."

"Looks like we got them nailed, boss."

"For the weed, at least. I'm not sure about the murders. But those are Angie's problem, come to think of it."

Dave walked up. "Looks like your case is coming together, Bo."

"Yeah, we can charge them with possession and intent to sell a couple tons of weed. But mostly I want them for the three murders up on Scotchman."

"Me too," said a voice behind him.

Tully turned. Angie was standing there. "I have to tell you, Bo, Dave is a terrific shot but I don't think he's an Indian."

Dave laughed. "And Angie, you don't look like any FBI agent I ever imagined."

Tully said, "While you two are chatting, I'm headed off to bed."

Dave said, "You sure you won't join Angie and me for a celebratory drink, Bo?"

"Too tired."

"What celebratory drink is that?" Angie asked.

Dave smiled. "The one you and I are having."

"And what are we celebrating?"

"Remains to be seen."

Tully stumbled off toward his Explorer.

25

Tully slept until noon the next day. Still lying in bed, peering up at his paintings, he thought about his next move. For one thing, he would send Lurch out to the island in the swamp to collect the watering cans and any tools he could find that might contain fingerprints. Next, he needed to find the guns used in the killings at the huckleberry patch. He would check with Pugh to see if he found any guns in the rigs at the ranch. Some silencers wouldn't be bad either. He needed to grill the driver of the moving van, who no doubt was connected to the buyer of the weed. He obviously intended to haul it somewhere. The big white pickup needed to be hauled into the shop and have the front bumper tested for paint matching that on Marge Poulson's car. His head whirled. He turned over and went back to sleep.

An hour later, he got up, showered and dressed, and drove down to McDonald's for his Egg McMuffin and coffee but had to settle for a Big Mac. Then he drove over to Etta's. She beamed at him. "Oh, Bo, I'm so glad you stopped by. You've been so busy lately I didn't know if I'd get to see you before I left."

He looked around the living room. Several suitcases were scattered about in various stages of being packed.

"You're leaving?"

"Yes, but I'll come back sometime. Moody, Simms and Cline has offered me a nice sum to do a little job for them. It's such a terrific offer I couldn't turn it down."

Tully shook his head. "I can't say I'm happy about it, Etta. We've been getting along so well. But I understand. When a big chance comes, you have to go for it."

"Oh, I'll be back in Idaho before the snow flies. Maybe we'll still have time for that trip up through Idaho. At least we'll be able to do our lunches at Crabbs."

Tully said, "What I came to tell you, Etta — the guy we thought was buried in the crawl space under the ranch house, well, he turned up alive."

"Wonderful! I told you I wasn't a fortune-teller, Bo."

She stood on her tiptoes and kissed Tully on the mouth. He felt it all the way to his

281

toes. A few years older and he would have died from it. "Good-bye, Bo."

Tully stumbled out the door and, grasping both handrails, made his way slowly down the steps.

He drove the Explorer over to the hotel to pick up Angie. She appeared exhausted. She pointed at the sun. "Doesn't that bright orb up there realize it's September? This heat is killing me."

"Something's gone wrong, all right. I blame it on the Weather Channel. If those weather people would stop fooling around with their satellites and stuff, we probably could get back to normal."

Angie smiled at him. "I didn't realize you were such a science buff."

Tully nodded his head. "Oh, yes. Except for algebra in high school, I probably would have been a scientist instead of an artist. I also had a problem with fractions. Every time I divided one half by one half, I ended up with one. It was crazy!"

Angie smiled. "What did your teacher say?"

"Miss Busbee? She said it beat the heck out of her too. She was also the volleyball coach. I was dynamite at volleyball so she gave me good grades in math."

Angie slid over closer to him and rested

her hand on his leg. He noticed she wasn't wearing her seat belt but decided to ignore the infraction. "I guess it all works out in the end," she said. "Sometimes, though, I wish I'd become a teacher. Of all the worthwhile professions, I think teaching is best."

"Better than catching criminals?"

"Sure. Maybe a good teacher prevents a lot of criminals, if she teaches them the right stuff. I bet half the guys in prison can't read. You ever notice how few smart criminals there are?"

Tully nodded. "I've told a lot of them, 'You can't be dumb,' but they never listen. Then they turn up dead or in prison."

Angie said, "So you think you can choose not to be dumb?"

"Hey, look at me. I tell myself all the time not to be dumb. How else do you think I got to be this smart?"

"I've wondered about that."

Tully came to an intersection, checked for traffic, and then drove through a red light.

"Do you realize you just drove through a red light?"

"Yeah, but I'm sheriff, remember."

Angie shook her head.

"So what's the plan here, FBI?" Tully asked.

"You're the smart one. You tell me."

Tully tugged thoughtfully on the droopy corner of his mustache. "I'm absolutely certain we have the bad guys locked up."

"By 'the bad guys' you mean the genteel chaps we picked up last night."

"Yes, beginning with Ray Porter, alias Crockett."

"You think Crockett is the mastermind?"

"Yeah, I think he's running the whole show. He probably ordered the huckleberry murders, not that his partners needed any encouragement. Whatever the reason for the killing of those three young guys, I don't think he had the stomach for doing the thing himself."

Angie nodded. "I was thinking about what Pap said, that there are only two reasons for murder — silence and money. It's pretty obvious the young guys didn't have any money. So what kept them working like slaves on those islands? They could have figured out some way to get out of there."

Tully thought about this. "You're right. Their bosses couldn't have had a gun on them twenty-four hours a day. They had to be there voluntarily."

"Right. And it wasn't their silence the killers were worried about, at least not entirely. The victims had to be complicit in the marijuana project."

Tully glanced at her. "And why would that be?"

"Because they were supposed to get a cut of the profits. They worked like slaves for nothing all summer, because there was going to be a big payoff for them come the harvest."

Tully turned this over in his mind. "You think so?"

"It's a theory. In the end, it's cheaper to kill them than pay them. They couldn't very well not pay them and let them go. They would have tipped us off, maybe just spilled the beans over the phone and then beat it."

Tully gave his mustache another tug. "You wouldn't think they'd fall for a scam like going out to pick huckleberries."

"Nobody said they were smart."

"At least one of them was smart enough to hit the ground running. That's Craig Wilson. He's still out there someplace."

"Without Wilson, we really don't have all that much," Angie said. "It would be tough even tying them to the marijuana."

"How about the moving van?"

"The driver could claim he pulled into the ranch to ask directions to somewhere."

Tully sighed. "Maybe Lurch will be able to match some of the bullets to their guns."

"Did you find any guns?"

"No! Why do you keep harping on details!"

Angie said, "Crockett would be the easiest to break, don't you think?"

Tully shook his head. "I doubt it. That would be a death sentence for him in prison, and he knows it. The other guys seem scarcely smart enough to tie their own shoelaces."

Tully pulled into his parking space behind the courthouse, and he and Angie went down to the jail. He introduced Angie to Lulu and then asked the matron to bring Ray Porter, alias Crockett, into the interrogation room. "You need any help with him, Lulu?"

She laughed. "He'll be right in, boss."

Angie said, "How do you want to handle this, Bo?"

"I suggest we start with the rubber hose and then go to the electric wires and battery."

"I'm serious!"

"I suggest we try to scare him."

"I'll let you lead," Angie said.

"No, you!"

Lulu brought Porter into the interrogation room. He was dressed in the standard orange jumpsuit. True to his sociopathic character, he was still quite amiable.

"Have a seat, Ray," Tully said, pointing to a chair across from him and Angie.

"Thanks, Sheriff."

"You're welcome."

Angie said, "You know, Mr. Porter, you're involved in five murders here."

Ray went white. "Murders! I never hurt anyone in my life! I need my lawyer!"

Angie went on. "Listen, Ray, you can have a lawyer anytime you want. You don't have to say one word to us. It might be helpful to your case if you do talk to us right now, but I'm not promising anything. It does seem at this point that you were involved in a plot that resulted in the murders of five individuals."

Ray looked as if he was about to pass out.

Tully said, "You see, Ray, you started a sequence of events that ultimately led to the deaths of six individuals, counting Marge Poulson and a guy named Stark. It really doesn't make much difference you weren't holding a gun. We know we can nail your associates, and once we do that, they'll give you up in a split second."

Ray put his face in both hands. "I have a splitting headache. Do we have to do this right now, Sheriff?"

Angie said, "We can wait until you're feeling better, Mr. Porter. But any help you give us will be helpful to you at your trial, which, by the way, won't take place here in Blight but in a federal courthouse."

"A federal courthouse!"

"Yes, the murders up on Scotchman occurred in a national forest, so the FBI has jurisdiction. You are involved in a federal crime."

Ray groaned.

"I know how you feel, Ray," Tully said. "Blight laws are fairly flexible. They might give you a little wiggle room. And if every defense fails, there's always graft. Alas, I'm afraid you will be at the mercy of hard-nosed Feds like Agent Phelps here. Play-by-the-book types."

Ray jumped up. "I feel sick!"

Tully nodded to Lulu and she took him back to his cell.

Tully sighed and leaned his chair back against the wall and asked, "Which of the other guys do you think runs the operation?"

Angie thought for a moment. "Well, we know it wasn't Stark. Bosses don't stand guard at night in a swamp. Of the other two, I'd say the bigger one, Kruger, Stanley Kruger. I suppose it could be the other one, Rupert Quince."

Tully shook his head. "No, not Quince.

Nobody named Quince ever gets to be boss, to say nothing of Rupert."

"You're probably right, Bo. I say let's grill Rupert first."

They had Lulu bring in Quince. Tully thought the orange jumpsuit looked like natural attire for him.

Quince sat down in the chair across from Angie. She said, "Mr. Quince, this is Sheriff Bo Tully. He has some questions for you."

Tully said, "Actually, Rupert, I get you because I'm not all that smart. The lady here gets to question the leader of the bunch."

Quince sneered. "What makes you think I'm not the leader?"

"Well, it's pretty obvious, isn't it?"

"You think I'm dumb, hunh! You should have left the cuffs on me, because for two cents I could grab you by the neck and squeeze the life out of you!"

"I know. That's why I've instructed our jail matron here to shoot you dead if you make the slightest move toward me."

Quince turned and looked at Lulu. She had her hands behind her back. One of the nice things about Lulu, she looked as if she wouldn't hesitate to shoot a person dead.

"So what do you want to know?" Quince asked.

"For starters, did you shoot the kid with the blue door on the red pickup?"

"What is this? A trick question? I was home watching TV when that dope was killed. Who drives a red pickup with a blue door anyway? That's enough to get anybody killed. Maybe you should ask Stark."

"Can't."

"Why not?"

"Stark is dead."

Quince was quiet while he mulled this over. "How did he get dead?"

Tully wanted to say, "He refused to answer our questions," but he thought Angie would raise a fuss.

Angie said, "He was standing guard out in the swamp and made the mistake of shooting at law enforcement. What was he guarding, Mr. Quince?"

Quince sighed. "I don't know anything about that. Since Stark is dead, I can tell you he's the one gunned down the kid in the pickup. I didn't have nothin' to do with that. But I ain't saying anything more."

"In that case, Lulu," Angie said, "you can return Mr. Quince to his cell and bring in Mr. Kruger."

Lulu took Quince out.

Angie switched off the tape recorder. "What do you think, Bo?"

"That we got zip. What do you think?"

She shook her head. "Zip is a bit excessive. He did indicate Stark gunned down Lennie Frick. Why kill Lennie if he didn't see them up on Scotchman right before the murders?"

Tully sighed. "How can we prove Lennie was even up on Scotchman? He told me he was and we have a fingerprint on a beer bottle. What more could you ask? They shot him because they recognized his vehicle, the blue door on the red truck."

"How do you know that?"

"Angie, you can be a real pain."

"Hush! Here comes Kruger."

Quince was big but Kruger would tower over him, big chest, big belly, big everything. He pulled out a chair, spun it around, and sat down astraddle it, his big arms resting on the back.

"It doesn't look like my lawyer is here yet," he said. "So I suppose the reason for this meeting is to tell me I'm about to be released."

"Not quite yet, Mr. Kruger," Tully said. "We just had a very interesting talk with Mr. Quince."

Kruger laughed. "Quince is an idiot. He blabs all day long. Nothing he says makes sense, which you must know by now." He looked relaxed but wary.

"Actually, he was quite informative," Tully said.

"You've got nothing on us, Sheriff, and you know it. Nothing! Nada! We happened to stop by a place where some jerk stored marijuana. And you try to pin it on us!"

"Suppose I tell you we have an eyewitness?"

Kruger's eyes turned into hard, mean slits. "You don't have any eyewitness because there wasn't anything to eyewitness."

Tully laughed. "You forget. One of your intended victims got away."

Kruger appeared about to leap over the table. "There were no intended victims! Nobody got away!"

Tully nodded at Lulu, who instantly stepped forward and tapped Kruger on the back. "C'mon, big guy," she said. "Back to your cell."

"I'll settle with you later!" Kruger growled, pointing a finger at Tully.

"Take a ticket. There's a long line."

After Lulu had returned Kruger to his cell, Tully shut his eyes, leaned back in his chair, and rested his head on the wall behind him.

"What now, Bo?"

"How do you feel about camping, Angie?"

26

The time Tully liked best in the mountains was early morning, with the sun rising through the trees. It had taken them two days just to find the trail to Scotchman Lake. The trail hadn't been touched by the Forest Service in years. Trees had grown up in the middle of it. Other trees had blown down and crisscrossed it from every direction. Scotchman Lake obviously hadn't been a popular destination for many decades. The scars of blazes that originally marked the route for Civilian Conservation Corps crews back in the thirties could still be seen on a few trees.

Tully had fired up his tiny backpacking stove before Angie had even opened her eyes. She poked her head out of the small green mountain tent. "Breakfast ready?"

"Almost. I've got the bacon nice and crisp and the potatoes and onions sizzling."

"Great. Let's see, for the past two days

we've had bacon, potatoes, and onions for every meal."

Tully grinned at her. "I'm also cooking pancakes this morning. I'll spread peanut butter and jelly on them and roll them up for our lunch. Doesn't that sound good?"

"It sounds delicious! And you better not be lying, Bo!"

"Would I lie to you?"

Angie laughed and then groaned. "I'm a single great ache from one end to the other. And I haven't been out of these clothes for three days!"

"I know."

Angie pulled her shirt up to her nose and sniffed. "Do I really smell that bad?"

"I wasn't thinking of smell."

"I'll tell you this, Bo. When we finally get to that lake, I'm going skinny-dipping and you better keep your back turned. The only thing I'll be wearing is a gun."

"Ha! From the sound of it, you'd think I'd waited my whole life to catch a glimpse of a naked FBI agent."

Angie stepped over behind Tully. "Hey, someone's coming down the trail."

He stood up and squinted against the sun. He could just make out a figure stopped on the trail. Twice the man looked back over his shoulder, as if trying to decide whether to run back up the trail or continue down.

Angie stepped out on the trail and gestured for him to come down. "Come on, Craig! It's okay! You're safe now. Nobody is going to hurt you!"

The hiker stared at Angie for a long moment. Perhaps because she was a woman, he plodded on down.

Tully flipped the skillet. The pancake rose a good three feet in the air, gradually turned over, and landed back in the skillet. Perhaps this artful maneuver also had a calming effect on the hiker. Nobody flips a pancake and then tries to kill you.

"That's the first time I've seen anyone do that," Craig said, walking into their camp.

"First time it's ever worked for me," Tully said. "So you're Craig Wilson."

"Yeah, and you must be Sheriff Bo Tully. I suppose you've come to arrest me."

"No, as a matter of fact we came because we need your help to keep three bad guys in jail."

"You have them all locked up — Kruger, Quince, and Stark?"

"Stark is dead."

"Wow!" Craig said. "That's a surprise. Not that I mind."

"We have Kruger and Quince in jail, along with another fellow by the name of Ray

Porter, aka Crockett, who may be the brains behind the operation. We need you to testify about what you know, in order to keep them there."

Craig slipped off his backpack and squatted down alongside Tully. "I saw Porter only once but I heard them talk about him sometimes. They'd kill me if they could. They already tried it once. I told the guys on the way up to pick huckleberries this was a setup but they didn't believe me. So when we started down toward the patch I was ready to take off. I was on the right-hand end of the line of us pickers. The instant I heard the shots I hunched over and ran like crazy. As I rounded the brush, something stung my arm but I hardly felt it. I ran until I couldn't run anymore. There was a thick grove of evergreens down a couple hundred yards and I hid there. They sent Stark down to find me but after a while he gave up and went back. Then I worked my way down farther and hid by the road until I saw the white pickup go by. I must have hid for another hour until I stepped out and waved down a logging truck."

Tully said, "That's about the way we thought it went down. I don't understand why all you guys didn't take off earlier. You could have built a raft and paddled off the island."

"Yeah, we could have, but they had promised us each ten thousand in cash at the end of the summer. All we had to do was cultivate the weed. We knew it was illegal, but I figured for ten thousand dollars I could take the chance. They were nice enough to us, except for Stark. Once Kruger slapped Stark senseless for punching one of the guys. They brought in great food — pizzas, tacos, burgers, milk shakes, anything we asked for. Used a big white boat to haul the stuff in and the grass out."

"Porter ever come out to the island?" Tully asked.

"Yeah, he came out just the one time. He was pretty slick. You could tell he was the boss of the operation, that he was the one with all the connections."

Tully smeared raspberry jam on a pancake, rolled it up, and handed it to Craig. The kid ate it as if it was the best food he had ever tasted.

Angie said, "Make me one of those, Bo!"

Tully picked up another pancake, smeared it with raspberry jam, and handed it to her. Apparently it was also the best food *she* had ever tasted. "So, Craig, why did you get

suspicious about the trip to pick huckleberries?"

Craig licked some jam off his fingers. "For
one thing, it was the day we were supposed
to get paid our ten thousand apiece. It was
something about their attitude. Suddenly
they had all turned stone cold. I'm pretty
sure they'd been discussing why they should
pay these four guys forty thousand dollars
and then have them running around bragging about it. It was probably Stark who
came up with the solution."

So Pap was right, Tully thought. This time
it was both the money and the silence.

It suddenly occurred to Tully to introduce
Angie.

"Craig, this is Angela Phelps, with the
FBI."

"Hi, Craig," Angie said. "I've talked to
your uncle. He's the one who told us how
to find you. You can't believe how happy I
am to see you."

"The FBI!" Craig choked out.

Tully said, "Yeah, the FBI, Craig. The FBI
will be looking after you from now on. The
murders were committed on federal land.
As far as your part in growing the marijuana, that occurred in Blight County, so
we get a piece of you for that. If Angie and
her FBI bosses agree, I think we can work

298

out some community service right there in the sheriff's office."

Angie said, "You help us convict the bad guys, Craig, and we'll look out for you."

"As a matter of fact, Craig," Tully said, "I just thought of a community service project for you. I need a new well dug."

Angie rolled her eyes. "So the Blight way kicks in!"

"Yes, indeed."

Craig looked back up the trail. "Just about anywhere is better than that lake. No wonder nobody goes there anymore. It's one scary place."

"So I've been told."

Three weeks after Etta Gorsich left town, human remains were found buried in the crawl space of a house being demolished two blocks away from hers to make way for yet another strip mall. So Tully had a new mystery to solve and a culprit to find. He thought he should phone Etta and tell her. Her vision or whatever it was had proven correct after all. Daisy found the number for Moody, Simms & Cline in New York.

When the receptionist learned he was a sheriff calling from Idaho, she put him through to a vice president.

"Etta Gorsich!" the man said. "Why, she's just down the hall. You don't happen to be the Sheriff Bo Tully Etta's been telling us about?"

"Depends on what she's been telling."

"All good, sir, all good. It's a pleasure to talk to you! We could use some of your Blight ways here in New York. I'll get Etta for you."

She came on. "Bo! What a pleasant surprise!"

"Etta, I just had to tell you — we found human remains in the crawl space of a house two blocks away from yours!"

"Oh, Bo, that's terrible but wonderful! Maybe I am a psychic! You don't mind hanging out with a psychic, do you?"

"Not at all, if that psychic is you."

"Are we still on for that trip up through Idaho next summer?"

"You bet, Etta. Just the thought of it will keep me warm all winter. See you then." He could hear her laughing when he hung up.

Brian Pugh walked in carrying a cup of coffee. "You were right, Bo. The Slade gang was staying at the old farmhouse on the other side of Cow Creek. Marge Poulson had rented it to them. She was probably headed out there to collect the rent when they killed her. Just down from the bridge we found tracks on a little side road where they waited for her. The tracks match those on the pickup. You think they killed her to keep from paying the rent?"

Pugh sat down, brushed some papers aside on Tully's desk, and set his coffee cup down.

Tully leaned back in his chair and clasped his hands behind his neck. "I doubt they were concerned about the rent, Brian. It was meant to get her off Ray Porter's back. She was calling too much attention to Ray and the ranch, and they were afraid the whole operation would fall apart if we started poking around looking for Poulson's body. We would have found the marijuana instead."

Brian said, "So Craig will testify the three of them murdered his friends and wounded him. Kruger and Quince are goners, don't you think, boss?"

Tully smiled. "That's exactly what I think, Pugh. And we can make a pretty good case Ray Porter was the brains behind the whole operation, including the murders. Angie will be ramrodding the murder case, of course."

"What about Porter?" Pugh asked.

"Angie may get Ray, too, if Kruger and Quince turn on him and claim he was the mastermind behind the murders. We've already got him for cashing Orville Poulson's Social Security checks. As soon as I found out Orville had left his driver's license at the ranch, I knew we had Ray for the checks. That was the money he was living on. I have no doubt Orville's hours, if not his minutes, were numbered when he

302

showed up back at the ranch. We've already got Ray for storing the marijuana at the ranch he was managing. So I think we can say good-bye to Ray Crockett alias Porter for a long, long time."

"Oh, I almost forgot something," Pugh said. He took a sip of his coffee.

"What's that?"

"We found three .22-caliber revolvers at the farmhouse and three silencers. I just gave them to Lurch to check for prints."

Tully stared at him. "Gee, thanks for telling me, Pugh!"

The following week, the weather cooled and Tully took nurse Scarlett O'Ryan fishing and camping on the Saint Joe River. The camping produced the first rain of the season and finally reduced the threat of forest fires. Scarlett turned out to be a terrific fly caster and taught Tully a whole lot of things he had never tried before. Not only was she beautiful, she was a nurse, and all nurses know CPR. When you're a forty-three-year-old man out fly-fishing the Joe for a week with a beautiful young woman, it's reassuring to know that if CPR should suddenly be required, you're with someone who can perform it.

The employees of Thorndike Press hope you have enjoyed this Large Print book. All our Thorndike, Wheeler, and Kennebec Large Print titles are designed for easy reading, and all our books are made to last. Other Thorndike Press Large Print books are available at your library, through selected bookstores, or directly from us.

For information about titles, please call:
(800) 223-1244

or visit our Web site at:
http://gale.cengage.com/thorndike

To share your comments, please write:
Publisher
Thorndike Press
295 Kennedy Memorial Drive
Waterville, ME 04901